MONSTER MAYHEM

GUY BASS

ILLUSTRATED BY ROSS COLLINS

To other Monsters

Scholastic Children's Books
A division of Scholastic Ltd
Euston House, 24 Eversholt Street
London, NW1 1DB, UK
Registered office: Westfield Road, Southam, Warwickshire, CV47 0RA
SCHOLASTIC and associated logos are trademarks and/or registered trademarks of Scholastic Inc.

Gormy Ruckles: Monster Birthday
First published in the UK by Scholastic Ltd, 2009
Text copyright © Guy Bass, 2009
Illustrations copyright © Ross Collins, 2009

Gormy Ruckles: Monster Contest
First published in the UK by Scholastic Ltd, 2009
Text copyright © Guy Bass, 2009
Illustrations copyright © Ross Collins, 2009

Gormy Ruckles: Monster Hero
First published in the UK by Scholastic Ltd, 2009
Text copyright © Guy Bass, 2009
Illustrations copyright © Ross Collins, 2009

This edition published in the UK by Scholastic Ltd, 2011

Cover illustration © Ross Collins, 2011

The moral rights of the author and illustrators of this work have been asserted by them.

ISBN 978 1407 13031 6

A CIP catalogue record for this book is available from the British Library.

Printed and bound by CPI Group (UK) Ltd, Croydon, CR0 4YY
Papers used by Scholastic Children's Books are made from wood grown in sustainable forests.

1 3 5 7 9 10 8 6 4 2

This is a work of fiction. Names, characters, places, incidents and dialogues are products of the author's imagination or are used fictitiously. Any resemblance to actual people, living or dead, events or locales is entirely coincidental.

www.scholastic.co.uk/zone
www.guybass.com

MONSTER BIRTHDAY

Meet the Ruckles

(If you dare)

Gormy Ruckles, the monster boy, was very small, very blue and very hairy. He had a long tail and just one quite good fang. Gormy lived at No. 1 Peatree Hill with his mother, Mogra the Horrid, and his father, Grumbor the Grim.

If you ever happen to run into them. . .

. . .keep running!

Happy (one eighth-and-an eighth) Birthday!

Gormy woke up just as the sun began to peek over Peatree Hill. It was the forty-second time he had woken up that night. Then again, he was surprised he had got any sleep at all – today was Gormy's birthday! And not just any birthday – today, Gormy Ruckles was turning *one-eighth-and-an-eighth*. As far as he was concerned, being one-eighth-and-an-eighth meant he was finally a *real monster.*

I wonder what I look like now I'm a real monster? Gormy thought, sitting up in bed. *I must be at least as big as my dad. No, bigger! I bet I have a hundred horns on my head, and tusks as thick as tree trunks. Or claws that drag along the ground!* He couldn't wait to find out.

Gormy leapt out of bed and delved into his Big Chest of Monstrously Excellent things. He rummaged past a smashing bone and a packet of dried snack-rats and took out a large, silver plate. As monsters don't have mirrors (most monsters look far too scary to risk looking at their own reflection), Gormy had spent two days polishing the plate so that he would be able to see exactly how monstrous he looked on his birthday.

Gormy held the plate in front of his face and stared at it. Oddly, he couldn't see a hundred horns. He couldn't make out any tusks or claws either, for that matter.

Maybe I didn't polish the plate hard enough, thought Gormy. He decided to go downstairs and check how he looked in one of the shiny saucepans. He rushed out of his room and bounced down the massive stairs. But as he was racing towards the kitchen. . .

Gormy bumped into his father! He looked up and saw Grumbor towering above him.

Grumbor was a huge, terrifying monster, with twice as many teeth, tusks and horns than were practical.

Grumbor had won the *Monster of Monsters Most Stomped Village Award* two years running, and had once roared an entire herd of cows to death.

"I was just coming to find you," said Grumbor, in a voice that sounded like fifty rocks being hit with fifty hammers. "So how does it feel to be one-eighth-and-an-eighth?"

"Small," muttered Gormy, wondering why he was still tinier than one of his father's toeclaws. He ran into the kitchen to find his mother, Mogra, making breakfast. She was just as big as ever too! Which was about as big as a garden shed, but much more hairy and pink.

"Happy birthday, Gormy! I'm just rolling some puppy pancakes. How about a glass of goatshake while you wait? I shook the goat fresh this morning," she said.

"What's going on? Why are you both still big? I mean, why am I still small? I'm one-eighth-and-an-eighth!" said Gormy in desperation. Grumbor laughed so hard that cracks appeared in the walls.

"It takes more than one birthday to make you a monster," he said. "What did you think, that you'd just wake up and be as big as me?"

"Well, I . . . no," lied Gormy, suddenly a bit embarrassed.

"Oh Gormy, you don't just change into a monster overnight. It takes years. You shouldn't be so impatient to grow up," said Mogra, handing him a pancake. "Here, I've put an extra puppy in it for you."

"Thanks," said Gormy, meekly. He couldn't believe how stupid he'd been. This was turning out to be the worst birthday *ever*! Even worse than the one where he lost his milk fang in his birthday cake! He slumped in his chair, feeling like the whole day was ruined.

"You should eat up," said Grumbor, swallowing five pancakes at once. "You'll need all your strength in the land beyond the hill."

"*The land beyond the hill?*" Gormy repeated, his furry blue lip quivering with excitement.

"Oh, did I forget to mention it?" said Grumbor with a monstrous grin. "We're going *fishing*."

How to catch a fish (with a rock)

Gormy couldn't believe it! He was going to the land beyond the hill for the first time ever (that is, apart from the time he had to go and rescue his sheep from a pack of wolves, but as that was a *very big secret*, it didn't really count). And what's more, he was going fishing!

Gormy had never even seen a fish before, never mind eaten one. Monsters always talked about fish in hushed, nervous tones, but Gormy had never thought to ask why. It certainly wasn't one of the sixteen questions he asked his father in a single breath.

"When are we going? Can we go now? Can Mike come too? Will I see any hoomums? Will we see a hundred hoomums? Will we see a *million*? How many is a million? When are we going? Where do we catch the fish? How do we catch the fish? How many fish will we catch? What does a fish look like? What *is* a fish? Is it like a bird? Does it have wings? When are we going?"

"Finish your breakfast," said Grumbor. "Monsters never go anywhere on an empty stomach. Then fetch your **How to be a Better Monster** book and meet me at the front door."

Gormy swallowed his breakfast without a single chew, burped politely, then ran up to his room. He got out his backpack and put his **How to be a Better Monster** book (which contained all six hundred and eleventy-six of his monstering lessons) inside, then rushed downstairs and out of the front door.

"Many happy returns, Gormy!" came a small, gruff voice. There, perched on a hanging basket (of

stinging nettles – it was a monstrous
house, after all) was Mike the
scuttybug.

Mike was Gormy's only
friend, and despite being
ugly, slimy and smelly, he
was the best friend a
monster boy could ask for.

"Mike! You won't
believe it – I'm going to the
land beyond the hill!" squealed Gormy.

"Great! Plenty of fresh, tasty dung in the
land beyond the hill," Mike replied, getting that
glazed look he always got when he thought
about his favourite food. "Mind if I tag along?"
he added, scuttying inside Gormy's backpack.

"Right, it's time we were off," said Grumbor,

emerging from behind the house with a truly enormous sack of rocks on his back.

"What are the rocks for?" asked Gormy.

"Fishing, of course," said Grumbor. "Can't fish without rocks."

Now more excited than ever, Gormy followed his father down Peatree Hill. They worked their way through the thick ring of trees that surrounded the hill and made it look, from the outside, like a scary forest. Finally, they reached the edge. Grumbor pushed a tree aside with his vast claws.

"What are you waiting for?" said Grumbor.
Gormy took a deep breath into three of his four
lungs, and clambered through.

He was in the land beyond the hill.

It was even more mind-boggling than Gormy
remembered! In fact, it was probably the most
boggled his mind had ever been. He stared out
across the endless valley. It was impossible to
see it all. There was every colour, shape and
smell Gormy could imagine. Cows and sheep
grazed lazily in lush, green fields, which spread
out as far as the eye could see. Tall trees cast
long shadows in the morning sun, and a warm,
welcoming breeze brushed across Gormy's fur.

Then, as his eyes darted in every direction,
Gormy noticed something else. It was a

hoomum village. He had never seen one so close-up before! There were small, wooden houses with thatched roofs, and more hoomums than he could count. They looked even stranger than he remembered – almost hairless, and covered in "cloves" to try and make themselves look less edible.

"Can I scare some hoomums?" he asked, with a monstrous glint in his eye.

"Absolutely not," said Grumbor. "You must *never* approach hoomums in the day. There are just too many of them. If they can see you coming, they'll have time to get together and attack *you*! That's why I usually only monster at night."

Gormy sighed. At this rate he was never going to scare a hoomum! Being one-eighth-and-an-eighth wasn't turning out at all like he had hoped.

"Don't worry, there's plenty of monstrousness to come – we're nearly at the river," said Grumbor as he wandered down the hill. Gormy scampered after him.

The river cut through the valley like a giant,

endless snake, and beneath its silvery surface,
Gormy could see dozens of brightly-coloured
creatures darting around as if they were late for
something.

"What *are* they?" asked Gormy, peering into
the water.

"They're what we came for! They're *fish*, and you can't go fishing without fish," chuckled Grumbor, taking an enormous rock out of the bag. "Now, watch and learn."

"This should be good," said Mike, poking his greasy head out of Gormy's backpack. Gormy and Mike watched Grumbor lift the rock high above his head. He waited for the right moment, took aim, and threw!

BOOOOSH!

Water and fish went everywhere! They scattered in their dozens along the banks of the river, flipping and flapping in horrid bewilderment. One even bounced off Gormy's head!

"Can I have a go?" squealed Gormy, jumping up and down. Grumbor poured the sack of rocks out on to the ground. Gormy grabbed the biggest one that he could lift, and waited for the fishiest fish that he could see. He took aim, and threw!

PLISH!

"I got him!" cried Gormy. Sure enough, a small, stunned fish bobbed to the surface of the water. It didn't look at all like he thought it would (it didn't have wings or a beak or anything). It didn't even look very tasty, not like a hoomum. Still, he *was* a monster, so the least he could do was eat it. He was just about to pop it in his mouth when. . .

"*Don't eat that!*" yelled Grumbor. His voice was so thunderous that it caused a small earthquake in the next valley. "That's a fish! Monsters can't eat fish! In fact, it's the only thing we cannot eat. Cows, sheep, hoomums, rocks – they're all fine – but not fish!"

"What happens if monsters eat fish?" said Gormy. He saw his father shudder, for the first time ever. Then Grumbor shook his head, and spoke a single word.

"*Croodles.*"

Croodles

"What's Croodles?" asked Gormy, nervously.

"Croodles is the worst thing a monster can suffer – a bellyache of monstrous proportions," replied Grumbor. "*Anything* can happen with a bout of Croodles. Absolutely anything! It is the one single advantage that hoomums have over monsters. Hoomums can eat fish. In fact, they love it! But we monsters cannot."

"I bet *you* could eat a fish, Dad," Gormy said.

"I tried, once. I was on a fishing trip, just like you. My father warned me not to eat it, but I wouldn't listen. I wolfed that fish down in one gulp. I thought I was the most monstrous monster in the whole world. But then, the Croodles began."

"What happened?" asked a wide-eyed Gormy.

"Let's just say it was the longest day of my life! There was nothing I could do except wait for the fish to . . . come out the other end. Lesson six hundred and eleventy-seven:

Monsters Can't Eat Fish. Not even me."

"Then, why do we throw rocks at them?" asked Gormy.

"Why? Because it's monstrous!" said Grumbor. Suddenly, he grabbed a rock and stomped down the riverbank, shouting, "Look, there's another one!"

Gormy stared at the fish in his paws. He couldn't believe something so small and unmonstrous could cause so much trouble.

"I bet *I* wouldn't get Croodles," he whispered, as Mike scuttied around his head. "Not now I'm one eighth-and-an-eighth."

"You're not thinking about what I think you're thinking about, are you?" said Mike, right into Gormy's ear, "because that Croodles sounds like a whole mess of trouble. If you're hungry, why don't I roll you a nice ball of dung?"

But it was too late. Gormy shoved the fish into his mouth and swallowed it whole! He waited a moment, half expecting his guts to explode ... but nothing happened. Not so much as a belly-twinge. Gormy couldn't believe he'd done it! He hadn't even got a *touch* of Croodles!

"I did it!" Gormy squealed. He immediately raced after his father, shouting, "Dad, Dad! I did it, I—" but he suddenly stopped. He couldn't tell his father that he'd disobeyed him on their first trip out. He'd never be allowed to leave Peatree Hill again!

"What is it? What did you do?" Grumbor asked, spinning around. His rock flew out of his hand, squashing a passing sheep.

"I . . . I did . . . nothing," muttered Gormy.

Grumbor shook his head. "Nothing? Why would you shout about doing nothing? Honestly, here I am trying to teach you how to be monstrous, and you're not even paying attention," Grumbor sighed, and began tramping back up the hill (picking up the squashed sheep on the way – he hated to waste food).

Meanwhile, Gormy couldn't believe what he'd done. He tried not to grin, but it was no good. He had to cover his mouth with both paws so that Grumbor didn't see.

Surprise!

By the time Gormy and his father got back to the hill, Gormy had decided that turning one-eighth-and-an-eighth was the best thing that had ever happened to him. He had turned into the most monstrous monster ever! He could even eat fish without getting Croodles! As he swung the front door open, Gormy was sure the day couldn't get any better.

"Surprise!" cried his mother. She'd thrown a party for him! Well, sort of. Gormy didn't have enough friends for an actual party. Also, Mike (who was understandably wary of being stepped on) had already scuttied off. But it was still very exciting. There was a banner strung across the ceiling that read "Happy Birthday Gormy" and Mogra was holding the biggest sack of presents Gormy had ever seen!

"Here you go, Gormy – many happy returns!" said his mother, handing him the sack. Gormy rummaged through it with glee. Inside he found:

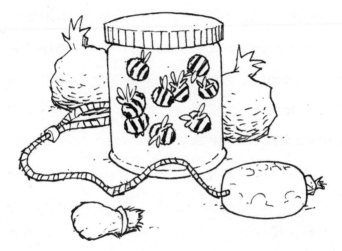

ONE LUCKY RABBIT'S FOOT
(to go with Gormy's lucky goat's nose and lucky cow's head)
TWO BAGS OF BOMB-SWEETS

(you never know whether
you'll get a sweet or a bomb. . .)
ONE JAR OF ANGRY BEES
(for eating, playing or writing with)
ONE ENDLESS SOAP-ON-A-ROPE
(a never-ending soap bar for keeping
monstrous fur clean and glossy).

Gormy was delighted! They were all perfect additions to his Big Chest of Monstrously Excellent things.

"Right, time for cake," said Mogra. Gormy followed his parents into the kitchen. There, on the table, was the biggest birthday cake he'd ever seen. It was at least eight times bigger than he was, and made from all his favourite things. He could see at least three goat's legs pointing out of it, and the top was covered in donkey's ears!

"I even added a touch of piglet, since it's a special occasion," said Mogra, cutting him an enormous slice. Gormy clambered up a chair leg and sat down. He grabbed the cake and licked his lips. . .

GRUoooOORBLE!

What was that? thought Gormy. It felt like a strange *bubbling* coming from inside him.

"Are you all right, Gormy?" asked Grumbor.

GRUoooOOorBLE!

There it was again, and twice as bubbling as before! It felt like Gormy's stomachs (the large one *and* the small one) were turning over and over! His head started to spin. What was going on?

"You've gone an awfully pale shade of blue," said Mogra.

Gormy felt the bubbling go all the way up his

body. He felt dizzy everywhere – even in his fur! He put a paw over his mouth – but it was too late!

It was a burp of truly epic proportions. In fact, it was so monstrous that it came out as a big, green cloud of gut-gas! It shot out of Gormy's mouth and landed on his mother's face! Mogra shrieked as the burp covered her in a cloud of green smoke and turned her whole face green.

"Eeek! I can't see!" she shrieked, as Gormy felt his stomach start to bubble again. He looked down at his blue belly, which was quivering like a bowl of badger custard. He felt the bubbling rise, and tried to clamp both hands to his mouth. . .

BUUUArrrP!

BErP!

BArP!

BORP!

BAAROOP!

BURiRUUP!

BUUUArrrP!

Bright green clouds of burp-smoke shot out of Gormy's mouth! One after the other, a barrage of belches blew across the room. And wherever they landed, a huge, green stain appeared. Grumbor took the brunt of the burps this time – on the elbow, on the ear, even one on his tail! As he dived for cover, Gormy fired another seven-and-a-half belches across the room. Within moments, the whole kitchen was filled with green smoke and covered in stains.

"What on Peatree Hill have you been eating, Gormy?" said Grumbor. "A polite burp is all very well and monstrous, but making a mess isn't!"

It couldn't be, not the fish! I ate it and everything was fine, thought Gormy. As his parents tried to catch the burps that hadn't landed yet, Gormy jumped down from the table and rushed upstairs to the bathroom. He closed the door and slumped to the floor. He had never felt so horrible!

As he lay there listening to his belly bubbling, Gormy realized something. It was such a horrible something to realize that he tried to pretend he hadn't realized it at all. But there was no escaping the truth . . . Gormy had *Croodles*.

5

A Tale of Two Tails

"What's all the racket?" said
Mike, waking up from a
nap on the bathroom
windowsill. "I was just
waiting here for
someone to go to the
loo. I'm *starving*!"

"Mike! You have to help me – I have

Croodles!" said Gormy, as the bubbling **GRUOOOOORBLE!** bubbled up in his belly once more! "Oh, no – here it comes again!"

But just as Gormy thought he was going to fire off another volley of brutal belches, the bubbling stopped! Gormy held his breath, waiting for something, *anything* to happen, but nothing did.

"Ha! Croodles shmoodles – see, you've beaten it already!" laughed Mike. "Croodles isn't a problem for a top-drawer monster like yourself, now is it? You swallowed that fish and you're already as right . . . as . . . rain. . ."

Mike trailed off. He was staring at Gormy, his buggy eyes even more buggy than normal.

"What? What's the matter?" Gormy asked.

"What's that behind you?" asked Mike,

sounding slightly curious and fairly shocked.

"I can't see anything," said Gormy, looking around.

"No, I mean behind you . . . on your behind!"

Gormy tried to look at his bottom. He gasped in horror! He had grown an extra tail!

"AAAAAH! Get it off! Get it off!" screamed Gormy, running around the bathroom.

"I don't know, Gormy – it looks fairly attached," said Mike, scuttying after him.

"What's happening to me?" said Gormy. He remembered what

his father had said, "*Anything can happen with a bout of Croodles. . .*" Gormy started to panic. "I can't let my dad see me with an extra tail! He'll know I have Croodles! I'm just going to have to stay up here and hide . . . at least until I can get rid of my tail!"

But the next moment (as is the way with these sort of things) there was a knock at the door.

"Gormy! What's going on? Are you all right in there?" said a voice as loud as fourteen foghorns.

"It's my dad! What am I going to do?" Gormy gasped, grabbing hold of his new tail. "If Dad sees this he'll know I ate the fish!"

"Not necessarily – maybe it's just a natural part of monster-boy development," said Mike.

"Do multiple tails run in your family?"

"No! I mean, I don't think so – although my Auntie Rogma does have two heads," said Gormy.

"Gormy! Open the door this instant!" yelled Grumbor. Gormy hopped on to the toilet just as his father barged into the room.

"What's going on? Why did you run off like that?" asked Grumbor.

"I just, uh, needed the loo," said Gormy, desperately trying to keep his second tail from whipping around.

"Well when you're *quite* finished, you can come downstairs and de-stain the kitchen! And don't forget your endless soap-on-a-rope!" grumbled Grumbor and then tramped off downstairs.

"How am I going to clean the kitchen without them seeing *this*?" said Gormy, holding his extra tail.

"Tuck it between your legs?" suggested Mike.

"Fat lot of help you are," sighed Gormy. He grabbed a towel and wrapped it round his waist.

 It stretched all the way to the floor like a long dress, covering his tails. "This will have to do until I can find a way to get rid of it," he added, and made his way to the kitchen, making sure to pick up his endless soap-on-a-rope on the way.

Blown Up

Gormy could hardly believe the state of the kitchen. Huge, green burp-stains covered the walls, the cupboards, even the ceiling. Gormy felt much

41

too dizzy to clean, but he couldn't let on that he had Croodles. He sighed a small, sickly sigh, tied the endless soap-on-a-rope to his wrist, and got to work.

Now the good thing about endless soap-on-a-rope is that it's, well, endless. It never wears out. It's quite a remarkable creation, but particularly hard to get hold of since Grumbor ate the only wizard who made it. Still, even with a never-ending supply of soap, it was going to take a while to get the kitchen clean again.

"I want this whole place *spotless*," said his father, coming into the kitchen. "Why on Peatree Hill have you got that . . . thing wrapped around you? It looks like cloves! Are you trying to look like a hoomum?"

"No, I—" began Gormy.

"Oh, Grumbor, leave the poor boy alone. Can't you see he's not well?" said Mogra, coming into the kitchen. Her face was still green, but she didn't seem to mind. "He's obviously caught a chill in the land beyond the hill. Fancy making him do chores when he should be curled up in front of a warm fire!"

As Grumbor grumbled suspiciously, Mogra took Gormy by the hand and led him into the sitting room. She put him on the sofa

in front of the monstrously big fireplace, and stroked his head with an enormous, pink claw.

"You wait here – I'll go and smash some wood for the fire," she said, and headed for the garden. Gormy closed his eyes and breathed a sigh of relief, but as he did so he felt another **GRUOOOOORBLE!** in his belly!

Gormy felt like he was going to burst. He held his stomach, first with one paw, then with two – then with both arms! It was then he realized that his belly was just too big to hold! He opened his eyes.

"AAaaahhh!"

44

He'd blown up like a balloon! And not just
his belly – his whole body was inflating! He was
almost three times his normal size, and
completely round. He tried to stand up, but he
just rolled off the sofa!

POMP!

Gormy landed on the floor, but instead of
just landing, he bounced! Gormy was floating
into the air! He was weightless! He bounced
POMP! off the wall, then **POMP!** off a
chair. He shrieked again as the ceiling rushed
towards him. . .

P-POMP!

Gormy bounced off the ceiling, which sent
him flying towards the mantelpiece! He was

heading straight for his mother's prized collection of fine bone china bones!

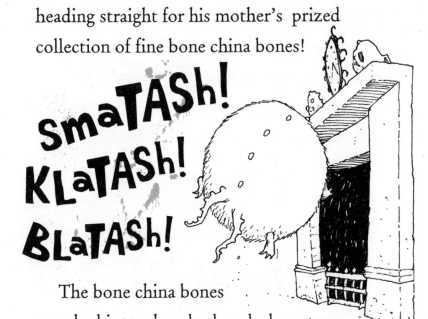

SmaTASh!
KLaTASh!
BLaTASh!

The bone china bones smashed into a hundred-and-eleventeen bony bits!

"Gormy! What's all that crashing?" called Grumbor. As Gormy **POMP! POMP! POMP!** -ed helplessly around the room, he heard his father's footsteps coming closer. He couldn't let him see him like this. This was even worse than having an extra tail. . . Gormy looked around desperately for somewhere big enough to hide a blown-up monster boy. Finally he spotted it – the fireplace!

That's my only chance! thought Gormy. As he floated towards a wall, he kicked against it with his tiny legs and shot towards the fireplace. He closed his eyes and hoped for the best. . .

POMP!

"Gormy? Gormy Ruckles, where are you?" came his father's cry. Gormy opened his eyes. Everything was dark. He managed to turn his swollen head upwards. He could see a dot of bright light above him.

He was in the chimney!

He'd made it! He'd managed to bounce into the fireplace and up the chimney. He was safe. He was hidden.

Unfortunately, he was still floating upwards. . .

A Sticky Situation

Gormy was floating towards the top of the chimney! He'd be at the top in seconds, and then what? He'd just float off into the air – no one would ever find him! *On the plus side,* Gormy thought, *I wouldn't get into trouble...*

Gormy reached out with his arms to stop himself but it was no use! His head was already out of the chimney when

BLUP!

He stopped.
Gormy was stuck!
His body had swollen
so much that it was
too big to fit through the
chimney.

Well, at least I didn't float off to who knows where, thought Gormy. As he stared out over Peatree Hill, he decided that, in a competition for the weirdest thing any monster boy had ever done, this would probably win. He was almost at the end of that thought when he heard the muffled sound of his mother below.

"Where can he have got to? He was here just a minute ago. He must be delirious with fever, the poor thing's obviously caught a chill. Well, don't just stand there, Grumbor – look for him! I'll get this fire going and warm the place up for him," she said.

Gormy couldn't help but smile. His mother was convinced that he'd caught some innocent, monster cold. She was even lighting a fire to keep him warm.

Lighting a fire?!?

He was going to be cooked from below! As his mother lit the tree trunk far below him, Gormy struggled to get free –

but he was stuck fast! Before long, he felt his furry feet getting hot. Gormy panicked, wriggling and squirming with all his monstrous might!

"Put the fire out! I'm warm enough!" he cried (forgetting that he was trying to hide), but he was too far up the chimney for anyone to hear him. Then, just as he felt the tips of his two tails start to smoulder, his belly began to bubble again. **GRUOOOOORBLE!**

Gormy's whole body began to shudder and shake. The pressure was building up inside him even worse than before! He felt his bottom rumble like an impatient volcano, and then

PAAAAARRRPP!

It was the most monstrously trump-tacular

fart ever blown out of a bottom! Gormy shot
out of the chimney like a furry, blue firework!

"AAAAaaAAAH!"

he screamed as he whizzed through
the air! He whirled, spiralled and
cartwheeled in every direction,
propelled by violent Croodle-
farts!

He whooshed over the
roof of the garden shed,
zoomed along the surface of
the lawn, and then shot up
between two tallish trees.

Finally, after what seemed like
a lifetime of fart-induced flying,

Gormy hurtled back towards the house, and straight at the bathroom window!

"Uh oh. . ." began Gormy.

SPWAT!

Out with the Bad

Gormy hit the window like a giant fumblefly! His swollen body flattened against it, and then immediately started to slide down! As it was a very long way down (a monster house is, of course, monstrously large) Gormy grabbed hold of the windowsill.

GLOOOORRRTCHLE!

The bubbling was starting again! Gormy held on for dear life, but with each gut-churning rumble his grip on the windowsill got weaker. As Gormy's head spun, he felt himself slipping. . .

"Gormy, pull yourself up!" came a cry. Gormy looked up. Through the haze of dizziness he could see Mike in the bathroom! The little scuttybug pushed open the bathroom window.

With the last of his strength, Gormy pulled himself up. He squeezed through the window and dropped –

PA-DOMP!

– on to the bathroom floor.

"Blimey, what in the name of the Great Dung Heap has happened to you now?" said Mike.

"It's the Croodles! I don't know what to do, and I don't know what's going to happen next!" said Gormy. Then, as if on cue, the bubbling started again.

GLUUURRRTCH!

"Here it comes!" cried Gormy, flapping his arms in terror. The bubbling filled Gormy from head to toe but it was worse than before! Then, before Mike's eyes, Gormy changed colour! First red, then green, then a sort of pale lavender, then orange! His eyes bulged out of his head and his arms spun around so quickly it looked like he might take off!

And all the time the bubbling

GUUOOOORRPLE!

got louder!

"Mike, run! It's bubbling to my bottom again!" Gormy cried. Mike dived for cover under the bathroom mat, as Gormy's bottom rumbled and thundered like an upside-down volcano. As the noise got louder and louder (and louder!) Gormy leapt on to the toilet!

SPUT-APPITY-PAPPITY-PA-PoOOOoooM!

It was a poo of truly monstrous proportions! The whole house shook! Windows rattled, pictures fell off the walls (including the half-haunted portrait of Old Uncle Gobog) and the only piece of Mogra's fine bone china bone collection that wasn't broken, shattered!

When the noise finally stopped, Mike poked his head out from under the mat, and there was Gormy, sitting on the toilet, looking exhausted.

"Gormy, you're *you* again!" said Mike. Sure enough, Gormy was no longer blown up like a balloon. Nor was he orange, red, or any shade of lavender. He'd even gone back to having just one tail!

"I feel . . . better. I feel good! Do you think I got rid of it?" puffed Gormy.

"Looks like it to me. Your dad said it would 'work its way through' in the end. Crikey, you should watch what you eat, in future – or stick to dung, like me!"

"Think I've had enough of dung for one day . . . and that's one poo that even *you* shouldn't eat. You never know what might happen," panted Gormy, staring at the impossibly monstrous poo in the toilet. He climbed up the sink to give himself a good wash (the endless soap-on-a-rope was still tied to his wrist, after all) and remove all trace of Croodles.

It was as Gormy scrubbed his left armpit that he realized something – he'd done it! He'd survived Croodles without his parents knowing he even had it! Maybe he was more monstrous than he thought!

"You know, Mike, I don't think this Croodles is all that bad! And once I flush away that Croodles-poo, my dad will never even find out that I ate the fish!" said Gormy. "Not a bad day's work, eh, Mike? Mike?"

Gormy peered over the top of the sink and looked down. Mike was nowhere to be seen – and neither was the poo! It didn't take Gormy long to realize what had happened. A sense of dread made his toeclaws tingle.

"He ate it . . . He ate the Croodles-poo!" cried Gormy, leaping out of the sink. He looked around for any sign of Mike. After a moment, he spotted something – a set of tiny, pooey footprints. *Scuttybug* footprints. Gormy followed them along the floor, then up the wall. Oddly, by the time the footprints reached the windowsill, they looked a lot bigger than the ones on the floor. What was going on? Gormy clambered up to the windowsill and stared out. . .

"AAAAAH!" screamed Gormy. He was met with a huge, monstrous head, at least fifty times bigger than him! It was a monster! An enormous monster – more enormous and monstrous than any monster Gormy had ever seen! It had vast, buggy eyes and long antennae, and its shell-covered head was slimy and green. In fact, when Gormy stopped screaming, the monster started to look rather familiar. A moment later Gormy realized who the monster was, and that actually, it wasn't a monster at all.

It was Mike.

Attack of the Fifty-foot scuttybug

"*Mike?* Is that really you?" said Gormy, leaning out of the window. Mike had grown to a more-than-monstrous size! He was almost as tall as the house!

"I . . . feel . . . funny. . ." said the massively monstrous Mike in a huge, gruff voice.

"I told you not to eat the Croodles-poo! *Anything* can happen! Now look at you –

you've turned into a monster Mike!" said
Gormy.

"My guts feel dizzy..." moaned Mike.

"You've got to hide! If my parents see you
like this they're going to realize what
happened – we've got to get you out of here!"

cried Gormy. He leapt out of the window, on to Mike's head. "Quick, run!"

Mike began to scutty as fast as he could down the garden, as Gormy desperately held on to one of his greasy antennae.

"Head for the ring of trees, we'll hide you there!" said Gormy. With Mike's new, giant legs, it took him almost no time to reach them –

he was going faster than a hurried horse! Gormy shouted for Mike to stop, but he didn't. He didn't even slow down.

SCRACRAAASSH!

Mike burst through the trees as if they were dry twigs! There was a moment of darkness, then they were out, into the land beyond the hill!

Again!

This time, the land looked strangely sinister to Gormy. Every giant scutty-monster step away from the house seemed to be a step into some vast, unknown wilderness.

"Mike, stop! We have to find somewhere to hide! We're going too far away from the hill!" shouted Gormy. But by now, Mike was too full of Croodles to even know what was happening.

The gigantic scuttybug stampeded through a herd of cows, who mooed their most terrified moos and ran in every direction!

Then, just as Gormy wondered if Mike was *ever* going to stop, he spotted a hoomum village in the distance. Mike was heading straight for it!

Gormy remembered what his father had told him that morning, about not approaching hoomums in the day – *"If they can see you coming, they'll have time to get together and attack you."* – Well, they'd be able to see Mike coming from a mile away! The hoomums would think Mike was a monster for sure! Who knows what they'd do to him?

"Mike! Turn around!" yelled Gormy (deciding it might even be worth getting into trouble with his dad rather than take on a *whole village* of hoomums), but Mike just kept running further into the valley. Gormy crawled up Mike's head to see if he could shout into one of his ears, but he wasn't even sure where they were.

What am I going to do? Stupid Croodles!

thought Gormy. Just then, he spotted the endless soap-on-a-rope, still tied to his wrist. He immediately had an idea. *If the endless soap-*

on-a-rope can clean the Croodle-burps, maybe it can clean Mike! he thought. It was his only chance to save his friend. Gormy took the endless soap-on-a-rope off his wrist, then began climbing up one of Mike's long antennae. It shook as Mike ran, but Gormy kept climbing, pulling himself along until he reached the end. Gormy stared ahead – they were almost at the hoomum village!

Suddenly, Gormy slipped! He held on with one paw as he dangled on the antenna, face to face with the monstrously massive Mike. The scuttybug's eyes were glazed over, and his mouth was wide open as he belched and burped. Gormy had a clear shot. He held on tight, and took aim. . .

"Hey Mike – eat this!" he cried, and threw the soap!

It landed in Mike's mouth and disappeared into his belly! Gormy tried to hold on, but he was still slipping. . . If the hoomums didn't get him, he was going to be trampled by his best friend!

Just then, Mike's expression changed. He started to shake from side to side, and bright pink steam shot out of his body in every direction! Then, as the steam poured into the air, Mike began to get smaller. He went from being as big as twenty cows, to ten, to one!

Gormy could barely see through the clouds of steam – he had no idea what was happening until he suddenly felt the touch of grass beneath his feet! He let go of Mike's antenna, and rolled

GLOMP! GOMP! GUMP!

along the ground! It should have hurt but after a bout of Croodles, Gormy barely noticed a few scuffs and bruises. He scrambled to his feet. In the distance, he could see the hoomums pouring out of their houses and grouping together. They must have seen Mike! They were coming to get him!

"Mike? Mike, where are you?" said Gormy. After a moment, he heard a tiny, gruff voice.

"Oi, watch where you're
standing – you nearly
squashed me flat!"

"Mike, you're you again!"
cried Gormy, looking down.
Sure enough, there was Mike,
back to normal and flat on his back.
Next to him was a small piece of rope, but
the soap had completely disappeared.

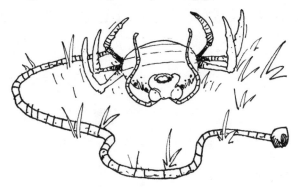

"Not so endless, after all," said Gormy. He
scooped Mike up and popped him on his shoulder.

"What happened?" asked Mike. "I hardly remember anything after eating that tasty bit of dung."

"I'll tell you all about it later, Mike," said Gormy. He stared back at the hoomums. Since Mike was small again, they could no longer see him, so they just ran about and shouted like headless Hop-gobbins. Gormy ducked down in the long grass before they noticed him, and began the long crawl back up Peatree Hill.

A Perfectly
Monstrous Birthday

It took Gormy and Mike quite some time to get back to the house. So long, in fact, that by the time they walked through the back door it was starting to get dark. Needless to say, Gormy's parents had noticed he was missing. They were waiting for him in the kitchen.

"Gormy! Where have you been? Don't you know what time it is? Have you seen the state of my bone china bones? What has got into you today?" Mogra said in one breath.

"No more nonsense, Gormy," said Grumbor, sternly. "You're going to tell us what's been going on, and I want the *truth*."

Gormy thought about thinking up a lie – he even looked for Mike to see if he had any ideas,

 but he'd already scuttied off. In the end, the only thing that he could think of to say was "Croodles". Grumbor almost fell over at the mention of the

word. Gormy confessed everything – eating the fish, the bubbling, the burps and the breakages – even the whole giant, monstrous scuttybug thing, which sounded like a lie, but wasn't. After he had finished, there was a very long silence.

"So you mean to tell me that you disobeyed me?" said Grumbor.

"Y-yes," muttered Gormy, his pointy blue ears drooping.

"And you mean to say that you ate a fish, got a bad case of Croodles, burped all over the kitchen, grew an extra tail, blew up like a balloon, got fired out the chimney, flew around the garden, *and* rode a giant scuttybug into the land beyond the hill?" continued Grumbor.

"Um, yes. . ." whimpered Gormy. He held

his breath and waited for the shouting to start
. . . but it never did.

"Well, that sounds like a perfectly monstrous
birthday to me, wouldn't you
say, Mogra?" said
Grumbor, grinning
from tusk to tusk.

"I couldn't agree more – what a monstrous
way to celebrate turning one-eighth-and-an-
eighth!" laughed Mogra.

Gormy couldn't believe it!

"So, you're not angry?" he asked, scratching his furry blue head.

"Why would we be angry? That was a very monstrous thing you did, dealing with Croodles all on your own," said Grumbor. Then he leaned down to Gormy and whispered in his ear: "You know, the truth is, I've never actually *had* Croodles. I had the fish in my hands, but when my father told me about Croodles, I didn't dare eat it!"

"You mean, you made it up?" said Gormy, more bewildered than he had ever been.

"I think you'll be quite the monster when you're older," said Mogra. "But there's plenty of time for that! Now, who's for birthday cake?"

Lesson six hundred and eleventy-seven:
Monsters Can't Eat Fish

After tucking into a few slices of cake (and a whole goat's leg), Gormy realized how tired he was. Everyone agreed that the tidying up could wait until tomorrow, so Gormy made his way up to his room. He was about to get into bed when he spotted his **How to be a Better Monster** book. He opened it up at the first blank page and stared at it. Even though he wasn't a proper monster yet,

Gormy had been pretty monstrous! He'd survived Croodles – and even his father hadn't done that!

Gormy took an angry bee out of his bee jar, and wrote: **LESSON SIX HUNDRED AND ELEVENTY-SEVEN: MONSTERS CAN'T EAT FISH**

Then he thought for a moment and added:
UNLESS THEY'RE <u>REALLY</u> MONSTROUS

I can't wait for my next birthday, thought Gormy. He swallowed the bee, and climbed into bed. He fell straight into a deep sleep, and dreamed of monstrous things – roaring, stomping, smashing . . . and fishing!

MONSTER CONTEST

A Monstrous Mood

It was a hot, sticky day in Janvember, and Gormy Ruckles was in a particularly monstrous mood. The trouble was, he just couldn't find anything really monstrous to do (and there's almost nothing worse than pent-up monstrousness). There was only one thing for it.

Gormy needed a jolly good *roar*.

He wandered around the house, looking for

someone to roar at. He found his mother, Mogra, in the pantry, collecting a couple of cows for a monstrous lunch.

Gormy's mother was hairier than any animal she'd ever eaten, and had so many teeth that it took two hours to brush them all. Gormy crept up behind her as quietly as he could. She didn't suspect a thing! He was going to scare her head off! Or at least loosen it. Gormy took two deep breaths into two of his four lungs and

ROOOOaaaaar!

"Oh, hello, my little puffball, I didn't see you there. Did you want something?" said his mother, not in the least bit terrified.

"I was. . . No," sighed Gormy, sloping out of the pantry. How could his mother not have been scared out of her fur? Gormy decided that he had roared at everyone on Peatree Hill so many times that his roar must have lost its scariness. He would need to find some other way of being monstrous.

Maybe I'll stomp on something, thought

Gormy. *Nothing says "I'm monstrous" like a really stompish stomp!*

Unfortunately, almost everything in the house was much too high for Gormy to reach, and far too big to crush beneath his tiny, blue feet. He made his way into the kitchen and took a monstrously large (and charmingly decorated) plate from the cupboard. He placed it on the floor and lifted his foot into the air. . .

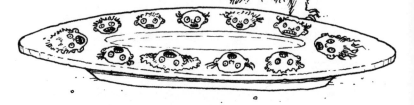

"I hope you're not thinking of stomping on that," said his mother, coming into the kitchen with a cow under each arm. "That plate was a present from your auntie Rogma. She painted the terrified hoomum villagers on it herself. You should know better, Gormy Ruckles."

"But I can't find anything monstrous to do! I hate being stuck on this stupid hill," moaned Gormy.

"Nonsense! There is *plenty* of monstrousness for you to get up to – you just need to use your imagination," said Mogra. "Have you tried in the garden? I could use some help with the weeding. . ."

"Weeding isn't monstrous!" protested Gormy. Actually, monster weeding *was* fairly monstrous, as monster weeds tended to put up a fight (it often took hours of stomping to beat them back into the ground) but that still wasn't enough for

Gormy. He tramped grumpily into the garden, looking for something properly monstrous to do. Maybe a really good *throw* would make him feel better. He spotted a plant pot, which looked ripe for a lobbing. He immediately grabbed it in both paws and lifted it into the air with a

GNnMMMPH!

"Oi! What's the big idea? I'm sleeping here!" said a small, gruff voice. Gormy looked up at the plant pot to find his best friend, Mike the scuttybug, clinging on for dear life.

As best friends go, Mike was surprisingly disgusting and smelly (even for a creature that only eats poo), but he was the only friend Gormy had ever had.

"Sorry Mike, I didn't see you there," sighed Gormy, placing the pot back on the ground.

"You all right, Gormy?" Mike asked, noticing how droopy-eared his friend was.

"I'm never going to be a real monster!" grumbled Gormy. "I should be out monstering in the land beyond the hill, not stuck here throwing flower pots."

"Cheer up, Gormy, you never know what's around the corner," said Mike, cheerfully. "I mean, one minute you could be going about your day as normal, and the next you might stumble upon a fresh pile of delicious poo!"

Gormy stared at Mike, a little confused. As much as he liked his best friend, Mike did seem to talk about everything in terms of poo.

"My dad'll find me something monstrous to do – *everything* he does is monstrous!" said Gormy, and began walking up the garden.

"Good idea," said Mike, following behind. "He'll know where to find some poo. . ."

Good News

Gormy spotted his father, Grumbor, by the garden shed, lounging on a chair and reading his favourite newspaper, the *Monster Gazette*. Gormy didn't even try to scare his father – Grumbor was much too monstrous to be scared by anything less than the sky falling on his head.

He was at least forty times bigger than Gormy

and eighteen-and-a-half
times as hairy, and
he had more
monstrousness
in one tail-spike
than Gormy
had in his
whole body.

"How's the monstering coming along?"
said Grumbor in a voice so thunderous that it
made Gormy's ears tremble.

"What monstering? Nobody's scared of my
roar, I'm not allowed to stomp, and I can't find
anything to throw! I might as well give up on
monstering altogether. . ." growled Gormy.

"Well in that case you certainly won't be
interested in *this*," snorted Grumbor, holding

up a page from the newspaper.

"*Cow Shortage Leads to Sharp Rise in Goat-Smashing*," Gormy read aloud.

"No, not that – the advert *underneath* it," said Grumbor. Gormy looked lower down the page.

JUNIOR MONSTER CONTEST

DO YOU HAVE WHAT IT TAKES TO BE THE MOST MONSTROUS MONSTER BOY IN THE LAND?

A DAY OF

★ MONSTROUS GAMES ★

WILL BE HELD TO DECIDE!

COME TO THE HALF-DEAD TREE IN GOBLOUSE WOOD ON

13th OF JANVEMBER

...AND LET THE CONTEST BEGIN!

Gormy could barely even stay on his two furry feet for all the excitement! A junior monster contest! He'd never even heard of such a thing!

"Still, if you're giving up on monstering, you won't want to bother with some silly monster contest. . ." said Grumbor, folding his newspaper.

"What? No! No, I didn't mean it!" squealed Gormy. "Can we go, please? I'll be the most monstrous monster boy ever, and I'll roar and stomp and throw and smash and crash and be *extra-* monstrous! Can we go, *pleeease*?"

"Oh, stop teasing the boy," said Mogra as she tramped across the lawn. "Of course you can go – we've known about it for ages. That newspaper is three weeks old! The fact is, we think you're ready for a *real* challenge."

"Lesson six hundred and eleventy-twelve: There's nothing like a bit of monstrous competition," said Grumbor. "Now run along and pack your backpack – we leave for the contest tonight."

And with that, Gormy's mother and father linked arms and stamped happily back to the house.

"See, what did I tell you? You never know what's around the corner!" said Mike, as they followed Gormy's parents indoors. "Mind if I tag along?"

"I'm going to a monster contest. . ." whispered Gormy to himself, not quite believing it was happening.

"Great! I'll roll some dung-snacks for the journey," chirped Mike.

3

The Journey to Goblouse Wood

Gormy realized that he had no idea what you should pack for a junior monster contest, so he stuffed his backpack with whatever he found lying around. In the end, he had packed:

- **ONE MOUSE'S TAIL**
- **FOUR BALLS OF FLUFF**
- **TWO AMUSINGLY-SHAPED STICKS**
- **ONE HOOMUM SHOE**
  (which **Gormy**'s father had got caught
  between his toeclaws during a village-
  stomping session)

He also packed his **How to be a Better Monster** book, which was full of useful monstering tips from all six hundred and eleventy-eleven of Gormy's monstering lessons.

"I hope you've left a scuttybug-sized space in that backpack," said Mike, rolling a dung-ball into the room.

"Climb on in!" squealed Gormy. "Just think, this time tomorrow I'm going to be the most monstrous monster boy ever! And I'll actually get to meet other monster boys! I might even make new friends!"

"I suppose," said Mike, scuttying into the backpack. "I mean, if you think you *need* more friends. . ."

"Gormy, it's time to go!" called Grumbor. Gormy grabbed his backpack and scampered downstairs. His father was already at the open front door, kissing Gormy's mother goodbye.

"You enjoy yourself out there, Gormy Ruckles," said Mogra, wiping a proud tear from her eye. "And remember, it doesn't matter if you win or lose – it's how you monster that counts."

"Bye Mum!" said Gormy, and raced after his father. The sun was setting as they clambered through the ring of trees that surrounded the house, and emerged in the land beyond the hill.

"There's no time to dawdle – it's a long walk to Goblouse Wood," said Grumbor, and scooped Gormy up in one of his huge, dark blue claws. He dropped him on the top of his head and said, "Hang on tight."

Grumbor set off down the hill at a monstrous pace! Gormy had never really had a Grumbor's eye view of the land beyond the hill before. It made everything look even more impressive than he remembered. This time, however, they travelled *much* further. Mountains that had once seemed far away now loomed right over Gormy's head, and torch-lit hoomum villages were suddenly so close that he could smell them.

By the time Gormy remembered to look back, Peatree Hill was nowhere to be seen. He trembled with nervous excitement, his head full of monstrous possibilities.

As dusk turned into night, Gormy yawned a surprisingly exhausted yawn. He wrapped his tail around one of his father's horns and nestled into his thick head fur. He drifted off, and his monstrous thoughts turned into monstrous dreams.

So Many Monsters

"Wake up, Gormy – we're here," said Grumbor,
stirring him from an excellent smashing dream.
Gormy rubbed his eyes in the bright morning
sun. He'd slept the whole night! He stretched
his tail and looked around. They were in a large,
circular clearing of a thick forest. In the middle
of the clearing stood a tall, menacing-looking
tree. It was white with no leaves at all, and had

been split down the middle by a bolt of
lightning. Its gnarled, coiled branches reached
towards Gormy like a hundred scary arms.

"So this is Goblouse Wood, eh?" said Mike,
poking his head out of Gormy's backpack. "I've
never been a big fan of goblice."

"What are goblice?" asked Gormy.

"Only the meanest, most monstrous insect you're ever likely to meet. They give the rest of us a bad name! Look, there's one," said Mike, pointing a tiny leg. On the edge of the clearing, Gormy could see a shiny, black ball.

"That's a goblouse? It doesn't look very mean to me," said Gormy.

"They're fine when all curled up and fast asleep, but if you manage to wake one up, then you're in trouble. First they cover you in snot-gobs to make you easier to chew, then *chomp* – you're lunch! Your only chance is to bop them on the nose – it makes them roll back into a ball!"

"I'd bop their brains out!" said Gormy, climbing down from the top of Grumbor's head. But no sooner had his foot touched the dusty floor of the clearing, than the ground started to shake and shudder! It felt like an earthquake! **BOOM! BOOM! BOOM!**

"**AAH!** What is it?" squealed Gormy, scampering under one of his father's toeclaws.

"Don't panic, Gormy. I think we have company," said Grumbor. As the sound got closer, Gormy realized it wasn't an earthquake at all – it was the sound of monstrous footsteps!

Suddenly, twenty-two terrifying monsters emerged from the wood! Each one was as different and frightful as the other. There were hairy monsters, slimy monsters, scaly monsters, and more! Some had arms and legs like Gormy, but others had tentacles, talons, and even flippers!

"So . . . many . . . monsters," said Gormy, as amazed as he was nervous. The twenty-two monsters climbed, crawled and slithered their way into the clearing. Before long, Gormy was surrounded by more monsters than he had ever seen. He watched his father shake claws with one of them as if they were old friends.

"Grumbor Ruckles, how on Butternut Hill are you?" the monster asked. It was huge, hairy and orange, and had three arms and three legs, but just one eye.

"Hello Brog! Mustn't grumble," grumbled Grumbor.

"Blimey, it's a right monstrous get-together," said Mike. "Shame there are no other monster boys here. But then who needs monster boys when you've got old Mike the scuttybug?"

"I . . . I suppose," said Gormy, trying to hide his disappointment.

"And you must be Gormy," said Brog Ump, the one-eyed monster. "I bet you're impatient to meet your competition."

Gormy watched in amazement as twenty-two monster boys appeared from behind the twenty-two monsters' feet! Each one looked like a miniature version of their father or mother, especially the three-armed, three-legged, one-eyed monster boy that appeared from behind

Brog's toeclaw.

"I'm Ruggle
Ump!" he
said. Ruggle
was by far
the biggest
monster boy in
the group, and he
towered over
Gormy. "And I know
who you are – Gormy Ruckles! I've heard *lots*
about you."

"You – you have?" asked Gormy.

"Of course! In fact, I heard that you're the
most monstrous monster boy in the land," said
Ruggle.

The thought of anyone thinking he was

monstrous filled Gormy with delight, but how could Ruggle have heard of him? He was about to ask that very question when

GROOUAOAAOO AAOAGHH!!!

"AAH!" shrieked Gormy. A roar like that could only come from the most terrifying monster ever!

"OH GOOD, THAT'S GOT YOUR ATTENTION!" boomed an impossibly loud voice. Gormy looked up at the half-dead tree. There, perched in a high branch, was the *least* monstrous creature Gormy had ever seen! He was shorter

than the shortest monster boy, and looked like
a piece of wizened old fruit with
fuzzy grey hair and a hat
that was so long it
dragged behind him.

For some reason, the other monsters (even
Grumbor) stared at him in silent awe.

"WELCOME TO THE ANNUAL JUNIOR MONSTER
CONTEST!" boomed the creature, clambering
down from the tree. "I AM YOUR HOST AND
JUDGE, THE OUTSPOKEN OOB!"

"Wow, the Outspoken Oob!" whispered Ruggle in amazement.

"Who's the Outspoken Oob?" asked Gormy.

"You've never heard of the Outspoken Oob, the monster mogul?" said Ruggle. "He's the editor-in-chief of the *Monster Gazette*! It's thanks to him that we have all these junior monster contests. Haven't you been to a monster contest before?"

"Um, yeah, loads!" lied Gormy.

"THERE WILL BE THREE ROUNDS TO THIS CONTEST! AT THE END OF THOSE THREE ROUNDS, I WILL DECIDE WHO IS THE MOST MONSTEROUS MONSTER BOY IN THE LAND!" bellowed the Outspoken Oob. "BEFORE WE BEGIN, ALL MONSTER BOYS SHOULD HANG UP THEIR BACKPACKS ON THE HALF-DEAD TREE. I LIKE TO

114

Gormy took off his backpack and went to hang it in the tree . . . but its branches were too high. Even standing on tip-claws, he couldn't reach the lowest branch!

"Here, let me get that," said Ruggle. He took Gormy's backpack and hooked it on to the branch.

"Thanks," muttered an embarrassed Gormy.

"No problem! I know we're competing against each other and everything, but there's no reason why we can't help each other out. I mean, what are friends for?" said Ruggle, flinging his backpack effortlessly on to the highest branch in the tree.

Did he say "friends"? thought Gormy,

beaming from ear to pointy blue ear. "Hey Mike, did you hear that? I've never had a friend before! A real, monster friend, that is."

"Yeah, he seems all right, I suppose . . . I mean, considering you just met him," said Mike, but Gormy wasn't listening.

"You'd better stay here in my backpack," he said. "There are a lot of monsters around and you don't want to get trampled. I'll come and get you when the contest's over."

"But I thought I was going to help. . ." began Mike, but Gormy and Ruggle had already raced off to the other monster boys, leaving him all on his own. Mike sighed a scuttybug-sized sigh and watched the monster boys gather for the start of the contest.

"THE STAGE IS SET!" hollered the Outspoken Oob as the monsters gathered around the tree. "AND SO, WITHOUT FURTHER ADO, LET THE CONTEST BEGIN!"

"Not so fast!" shrieked a horribly familiar voice. "I want to enter the contest too!"

Gormy knew immediately who it was. His excitement turned to horror more quickly than his mother could turn a cow into cow pie. Emerging from the crowd was his archenemy, the most horrible monster boy in the entire world.

His name was Poggy Boggles.

The Return of Poggy Boggles

Gormy's mouth dropped open at the sight of Poggy Boggles and his monstrously fat mother, Volga.

Poggy was Gormy's next-valley neighbour, and until today, the only other monster boy he'd ever met. Poggy was green, hairy, and so horrible that he made goats seem friendly. All Poggy ever talked about was how incredibly big and monstrous he was, except when he was telling everyone how incredibly small and unmonstrous Gormy was.

"Look, Mummy, there's Gormy Ruckles," said Poggy with a sneer, and threw his backpack easily on to a branch halfway up the half-dead tree. "He's still as tiny as ever, I see! Aren't you *ever* going to grow, Gormy? I've grown a whole inch-and-an-eighth since breakfast!"

"Size isn't everything, Poggy," said Ruggle, looming menacingly over him. Poggy nearly jumped out of his fur! He quickly shuffled behind his mother's fat ankle without another word.

"Ruggle, that was great! I don't think I've ever seen him actually shut up before!" said Gormy.

"Oh, don't worry about Poggy," said Ruggle. "I met him at the last junior monster contest, and he was just as much of a pain in the tail then. But he's all talk – he's not monstrous enough to beat us."

"Monster boys, line up for round one," boomed the Outspoken Oob. "Parents and guardians, kindly take a seat by the trees and try not to sit on any goblice."

"I've been practising for this contest every day for the last three weeks! How long have you been practising, Gormy?" asked Poggy.

"I. . . Um, well—" began Gormy, suddenly wishing that his parents hadn't kept the contest a surprise.

"When you're as monstrous as Gormy, you don't need to practise," said Ruggle. "What counts is how monstrous you are in the contest, right Gormy?"

"Right!" said Gormy, so confidently that he almost believed it himself.

6

Round one: Roaring

With the monster boys all gathered together in the clearing, the Outspoken Oob announced the first round of the contest – roaring!

"How's *your* roar, Gormy? Pretty monstrous, I'll bet," said Ruggle.

"Ha! Gormy couldn't roar his way out of a paper bag!" scoffed Poggy.

"Speaking of paper bags, here – take one of

these," said Ruggle, holding out a small paper bag full of sweets. "They're called boom-sweets. They make your roar extra loud and monstrous."

Gormy eagerly took one of the boom-sweets and popped it in his mouth.

It tasted like rotten eggs and sweaty feet – delicious! As he chewed away, he noticed the Outspoken Oob disappear around the half-dead tree, emerging on the other side with *another* Oob! She was as slow as a Low-Legged

Shuffle-Off, and so old and dry that she looked like she might turn to dust at any moment.

"I CALL THIS ROUND THE 'ROAR-SHOCK TEST'!" cried the Outspoken Oob. "THIS IS MY GRANDMOTHER, THE ANCIENT OOB! SHE IS A THOUSAND YEARS OLD, AND STONE DEAF! SHE CAN'T HEAR ANYTHING SHORT OF A THUNDERCLAP! THE MONSTER BOY WHO ROARS LOUDLY ENOUGH FOR MY GRANDMOTHER TO HEAR IS THE WINNER!"

As Gormy waited for his turn, he watched to see if the Ancient Oob would hear any of the roars. And what impressive roars they were!

ROARGH!

after

GRaAGH-H!

after **ROoOORRg!**

and even one

BROoOOoooOooG!

Each one was as remarkably monstrous as the last. But the Ancient Oob just sat there, saying things like "SORRY DEAR, DIDN'T CATCH A WORD OF THAT!" and "YOU'LL HAVE TO SPEAK UP!"

"Your turn, Gormy. Show them how it's done!" said Ruggle. Gormy thought that maybe, just maybe he could out-monster Poggy. Maybe he could out-monster everyone! He planted himself in front of the Ancient Oob, took the deepest breath he'd ever taken and. . .

"**Squeak!**"

It wasn't a roar at all! Gormy barely even made a noise! The Ancient Oob shrugged in disappointment. Gormy looked around in horror as the other monster boys began to laugh. Where had his roar gone? This had never happened to him before. He took another breath (this time using his spare lung as well) and. . .

"**Squeeeak!**"

It was even tinier than before! Gormy slapped his paw over his mouth as the other monster boys fell about laughing!

"Gormy, what's wrong? Are you OK?" asked Ruggle.

Gormy tried to answer, but all that came out of his mouth was, **"Squeak! Squeak! Squeak!"**

"GORMY RUCKLES IS DISQUALIFIED FROM THE ROARING CONTEST FOR FAILING TO ROAR!" bellowed the Outspoken Oob. Out of the corner of his eye, Gormy saw his father sigh and shake his head.

"Disqualified? Dear oh dear, I've never seen anything less monstrous in all my days," chuckled Mrs Boggles.

"Not to worry, Grumbor, some monster boys need more training than others," said Brog Ump. "I could always get my Ruggle to give Gormy a monstering lesson or two."

With the sound of defeat ringing in his

pointy blue ears, Gormy sloped off. He couldn't believe it! His first monster contest ever, and he'd messed it up! He looked back to see Poggy Boggles staring right at him and grinning a particularly monstrous grin.

Round Two: Stomping

Gormy sat under the half-dead tree, trying to work out what on Peatree Hill had happened to his roar.

"What was that all about, Gormy? I've never heard you roar so . . . *squeakily* before," said a concerned Mike from Gormy's backpack.

"I don't know, it just wasn't there! And I was so sure I could do it. . ." muttered a dejected

Gormy. "Ruggle must think I'm the least monstrous monster *ever.*"

"You're a great monster! You just need to believe it, that's all. Anyway, who cares what Ruggle thinks?" said Mike.

"I care! This was my one chance to make a real monster friend," sighed Gormy. "He even gave me a boom-sweet . . . I'd be surprised if he'll even talk to me now."

"Boom-sweets, eh? Never heard of them. I wonder if—" began Mike, but Ruggle came bounding towards them, wearing the **Most Monstrous Roar** medal. As it turned out, Ruggle's roar had been twice as loud as anyone else's, and the only one that the Ancient Oob could hear. As bad as Gormy felt, he was pleased that the best monster had won.

"Come on, Gormy, the next round is starting — the stomping contest! If what I hear is true, you'll win easily!" said Ruggle.

Gormy was an excellent stomper. He could smash through a stomp-stone in twelve seconds flat, and once accidentally sleep-stomped his bed clean in half. If he was going to prove his monstrousness, he was going to do it by stomping.

Gormy joined Ruggle and the other monster boys. The Outspoken Oob was waiting with a large bag. He reached in, and pulled out a small, multi-coloured sock.

"Welcome to round two — 'The Stomp Romp'! I have in my hand a 'stomp-sock'. It was knitted from the toughest materials known to monster-kind! There is one sock

FOR EACH OF YOU, LABELLED WITH YOUR NAME. THE OBJECT OF THIS ROUND WILL BE TO KEEP STOMPING UNTIL YOU HAVE STOMPED *THROUGH* YOUR STOMP-SOCK! THE MONSTER BOY WHO STOMPS THROUGH HIS SOCK THE FASTEST IS THE WINNER!"

Gormy couldn't remember ever having anything with his name on before, never mind his own stomp-sock! He waited eagerly for his turn to rummage in the sock bag, but when he finally got there, his sock was nowhere to be found.

"I think *this* one's yours, Gormy," said Poggy, dangling Gormy's stomp-sock under his nose. "I found it when I was looking for mine. I didn't even need to read the label – your sock was the smallest one in the bag!"

"Thanks," grumbled Gormy, taking the sock. It was striped in green and purple and had the words **GORMY RUCKLES** written on it.

"Anyway, I hope you have more luck with your stomp than your roar – I've never heard such a pitiful squeak!" added Poggy with a sneer.

"And who's going to beat him? I don't see *you* wearing a medal, Poggy," chuckled Ruggle.

"Oh yeah? Well maybe I – I – oh, forget it!" huffed Poggy. Gormy had never seen him lost for words before! It was better than brilliant!

"Monster boys, don your stomp-socks!" cried the Outspoken Oob. Gormy squeezed his furry blue foot into his stomp-sock. He was immediately surprised at how uncomfortable it was. At first it started to itch, and then it started to get hot. In fact, it got hotter and itchier (and itchier and hotter!) until Gormy thought his foot was on fire! He tried to wiggle his toeclaws around, but that just made it worse!

"Prepare to stomp!" yelled the Outspoken Oob. "On your marks, get set—"

"YoOOOOOOoWW!!!" screamed Gormy. His foot was red-hot! He hopped around the clearing like a horribly hysterical hop-gobbin!

"Hah! Call that stomping?" sniggered Poggy.

"Gormy, stop! What's the matter?" said Ruggle as Gormy barrelled into him.

"Hot! hot! HOT!" cried Gormy, bouncing around like a spring-footed Gallumpher! He couldn't help it, his foot felt hotter than a dragon's breath as he rebounded off the other monster boys, knocking them down or sending them flying!

"That boy doesn't know the first thing about stomping! He obviously needs more lessons!" guffawed Mrs Boggles.

"I'm *sure* Ruggle would be happy to give Gormy a monstering lesson or two, Grumbor," added Brog Ump.

"No thank you!" roared Grumbor, and started chasing Gormy around the clearing, doing his best not to trample any monster boys on his way. Finally, as Gormy hopped high into the air screaming "Hot! Hot!" Grumbor caught him by the tail. As he hung in mid-air, Gormy managed to pull off his stomp-sock.

"My foot! It's on fire!" yelled Gormy.

"What do you mean? It doesn't *look* like it's on fire," said Grumbor. Gormy looked down at his foot. Sure enough, it looked just like a foot should – blue and hairy with three claws at the end! What's more, it now felt completely normal, and not in the least bit hot.

"I don't understand. . ." murmured Gormy.

"Gormy Ruckles is disqualified from the stomping contest, for failing to stomp . . . and for unmonstrous silliness!" bellowed the Outspoken Oob.

Gormy was so ashamed that he couldn't bring himself to look at the other monster boys, but he could hear their laughter rumble through the trees.

"Honestly Gormy, I don't know what's got into you. You know that's not how you stomp!" barked Grumbor. "We'll talk about this when the contest is over. There's only one round left and I *insist* you don't make any more trouble."

Gormy was about to protest, but he saw that
look in his father's eye which told him that he
was better off biting his lip. As he
shuffled back to the half-dead
tree, Gormy wondered if he
had been wrong all along.
Maybe he just wasn't
meant to be a monster. . .

Round Three: Throwing

Gormy sat under the half-dead tree and stared at his stomp-sock. How could it have made his foot feel so hot? Then again, it was a *monstrous* sock. Gormy wondered if perhaps he just wasn't monstrous enough to wear it. In fact, he wondered if he was monstrous enough to be a monster at all.

"Let me take a look at that stomp-sock," said

Mike from Gormy's backpack. "I reckon there's something funny going on with this monster contest. First your roar, now this! It's as though someone wants to ruin your chances, and I think I might know who. . ."

"What do you know? You're not even a monster," said Gormy grumpily and threw the stomp-sock into the woods. "I got disqualified! Again! I'm useless!"

"Ha! You said it!" laughed Poggy as he strode over. "Poor Gormy, why don't you scurry home and leave the *real* monsters to it?"

"Oh, put a stomp-sock in it, Poggy. Where's *your* stomping medal?" said Ruggle, emerging from behind the tree wearing the **Most Monstrous Stomp** medal. As an embarrassed Poggy scurried off, Ruggle noticed how forlorn

Gormy looked. "Cheer up, Gormy, round three is about to start, and if you're half as good at throwing as I heard, you should win this round easily!" said Ruggle.

There was no doubt Gormy could throw. He could hit a goat with a log at thirty paces, and once threw a pebble so high that it came down with snow on it. It was Gormy's last chance to prove that he belonged in the contest.

"Yeah. . . You're right! I'll throw that rock into next week!" said Gormy.

"Gormy, wait!" called Mike, but Gormy and Ruggle had already joined the other monster boys gathered around the Outspoken Oob.

"Round three – 'the rock chuck'!" hollered the Outspoken Oob, pointing out a long line of twenty-four identical rocks. "These

ARE YOUR THROWING ROCKS! EACH ONE IS LABELLED WITH YOUR NAME. YOU WILL TAKE TURNS TO THROW, AND THE MONSTER BOY WHO THROWS THE FURTHEST IS THE WINNER!"

As he watched the other monster boys throw their rocks, Gormy knew this was his last chance to show Ruggle, and everyone else, how monstrous he was. He stood behind his rock. It was grey and round, with **GORMY RUCKLES** written on it. All in all, it looked thoroughly throwable. He grabbed it tightly, but it felt rather sticky, and left a rock-coloured stain on his hands.

That's weird, thought Gormy. *I didn't know you could get sticky rocks. Still, who knows what rocks feel like this far away from Peatree Hill?*

Gormy lifted the rock over his head. It wasn't even that heavy – this was going to be easy! He reached back and was about to throw when, all of a sudden, he felt the rock move. He looked up, and saw two long antennae pointing back at him.

"**Aaaaah!!**" Gormy screamed, and dropped the rock!

It immediately began to uncurl. Within moments, it was clear that Gormy's rock wasn't a rock at all.

It was a goblouse!

When Goblice Attack!

Gormy watched in horror as the goblouse uncurled to its full size. It was almost as big as a cow and several hundred times more monstrous. Gormy didn't even have time to wonder why it looked just like his throwing rock before the voice of the Outspoken Oob boomed out over the clearing.

"GORMY RUCKLES IS DISQUALIFIED FROM THE

THROWING CONTEST, ON THE GROUNDS OF NON-
ROCK THROWING AND BLATANT GOBLOUSE ABUSE!"

"Fancy bringing a goblouse to a throwing
contest! That monster boy should be banned
from the contest! In fact, ban him from
monstering altogether!" screeched Mrs Boggles.

"I *really* think you should let Ruggle give
him a monstering lesson," said Brog Ump, but
Grumbor wasn't listening.

"Gormy! It'll eat you alive! Run!" he cried,
leaping to his feet.

"Eat me?" squealed Gormy, as the goblouse
hissed in rage. The monster boys screamed and
ran in every direction! This, in turn, made the
grown-up monsters panic, and run into the
clearing to rescue their children. Within
moments it was a sea of giant, stamping monster

legs and running, screaming monster boys. But that didn't stop the goblouse from charging towards Gormy. Gormy decided that he should do exactly as his father said – run!

"Watch out for snot-gobs!" cried Grumbor, desperately trying to reach Gormy through the sea of monsters. Sure enough, the goblouse started firing sticky balls of yellow snot at

Gormy! **SPUT! SPUT! SPUT! SPUT!**

Gormy raced between the snot-gobs and the stampeding legs of the giant monsters trying to rescue their children. He ducked and dodged frantically, as a few misfired gobs splattered other monster boys, **SPUT! SPUT!** covering them in thick, yellowy goo.

Then, suddenly **SPUT!** A snot-gob hit Gormy on the back of the head! He fell to the floor, dazed and confused.

By the time he knew what had happened, the goblouse had zigzagged between the mess of monsters' legs, and was about to pounce on him! Gormy held his breath and prepared for the worst. . .

"Hang on, Gormy!" came a cry. It was Poggy! He pushed Gormy out of the way, and the goblouse landed on him instead! The goblouse fired a dozen snot-gobs right in Poggy's face, making him an easy to swallow snack!

SPUT! SPUT! SPUT! SPUT! SPUT! SPUT! SPUT! SPUT! SPUT! SPUT! SPUT! SPUT! SPUT! SPUT! SPUT! SPUT! SPUT! SPUT!

"Somebody help my little Poggy-woggy!" shrieked Mrs Boggles as she tried to push her way through the monsters.

"Hey, goblouse! Over here!" cried Gormy, kicking the goblouse in the bottom. The goblouse spun around and let out an ear-piercing hiss!

"Uh-oh," said Gormy, wishing he'd thought through taking on an angry goblouse! He turned and ran for the half-dead tree.

It'll never be able to follow me all the way up there! Gormy thought. He leapt on to the trunk, dug in his claws and started climbing, all the while trying to avoid the goblouse's snot-gobs. After a few moments however, the snot-gobs stopped, and Gormy looked back. The goblouse was climbing the tree! He was right behind him!

"AAH!" screamed Gormy, climbing twice as fast as he'd ever climbed! This time, Gormy didn't look back, he climbed and climbed until he was almost at the top of the tree.

"Gormy, this way! Up here!" said a small, gruff voice. Gormy looked up. There, in the very highest branch of the tree, was Mike! He was poking his head out of

Ruggle's backpack, which dangled from a thin branch. With the goblouse hot on his furry heels, Gormy clambered on to the branch.

"Crawl to the end! That fat goblouse is too heavy to follow," said Mike. Gormy pulled himself nervously to the end of the branch, hanging on tightly with his claws and tail.

"What are you doing way up here? And in Ruggle's backpack?" asked Gormy, trying not to look down.

"Just doing a little detective work," said Mike. "After what happened to your roar and your stomp, I got to thinking that a certain someone was trying to make you *lose* the contest . . . but I needed proof, so I climbed up here and – look out!" As Mike yelled, Gormy spun around to see the goblouse scramble on to the branch!

"Go away, this branch is full!" cried Gormy. As the goblouse crawled towards them, the branch began to bend and bow under its weight. Ruggle's backpack slipped to the very end of the branch.

"Hang on, Mike!" said Gormy, reaching out to grab the backpack. His claws brushed against the backpack, but it was too late – it slipped off the branch, and fell!

10

Ruggle's Backpack

"Mike!" cried Gormy as Ruggle's backpack crashed to the ground! He turned around to climb back up the branch, but the goblouse was blocking his path. It snapped its jaws and edged closer . . .

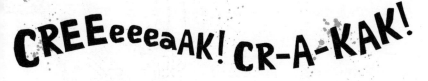

CREEeeeaAK! CR-A-KAK!

"Stop!" cried Gormy, as the branch cracked and splintered. "The branch is going to—"

SNAP!

"**AAAAAAAAH!**" Gormy screamed as he fell, expecting to hit the ground. . .

But instead he landed with a **FLUMP** in his father's paw – Grumbor had caught him!

Of course, nobody tried to catch the goblouse, which landed right on top of the backpack!

"Oh no! Mike!" shouted Gormy as he leapt out of his father's paw. By the time he'd reached the goblouse it was back on its feet and angrier than ever.

"Gormy, stop!" cried Grumbor, but Gormy was filled with monstrous rage. As the goblouse went to pounce, he took a deep breath and,

GROOOAAARRGGH!!!

It was the biggest roar he'd ever done, and easily the loudest roar of the contest! The goblouse was almost scared out of its shell, and froze to the spot in terror. Gormy didn't waste any time – remembering what Mike had told him, he lifted his best stomping leg and **BLOMP!** stomped on the goblouse's head, making it curl up into a ball!

"Mike, can you hear me?" he cried, carefully emptying the backpack on to the ground. There, among a host of objects, was his best friend, looking squashed but otherwise intact. Gormy placed him gently in his paw. "Are you OK?"

"Never . . . better. . ." groaned Mike, rubbing his head.

"I thought you'd been squished!" said Gormy, trying not to cry in front of the monsters who had gathered round.

"Oh, it'll take more than a fall from a great height and being sat on by a giant, monstrous insect to knock old Mike out of action," said Mike, then spotted the contents of Ruggle's backpack lying on the ground. "Still, now that I've finally got your attention, look!"

Gormy stared at the strange array of objects. They included:

- **ONE BAG OF SQUEAK-SWEETS, FOR THE TEMPORARY REMOVAL OF ROARS**
- **ONE JAR OF BURNING BLISTER**

BERRIES, FOR MAKING THINGS FEEL
EXTREMELY HOT, EVEN THOUGH
THEY'RE NOT

- TWO TINS OF "ROCK-COLOURED"
PAINT, FOR MAKING THINGS THAT
AREN'T ROCKS LOOK A LOT LIKE
ROCKS (especially goblice)
- ONE FOLDED PIECE OF PAPER WITH
THE WORDS "HOW TO STOP GORMY
RUCKLES WINNING THE MONSTER
CONTEST" WRITTEN ON IT.

"I. . . I don't understand," said Gormy.

"This is what I've been trying to tell you. It was *Ruggle* who made you mess up the contest!" said Mike.

"Ruggle? It can't be. . ." said Gormy.

"Who me? Rubbish! I've never seen any of those things

before!"shouted Ruggle, suddenly sweating nervous, yellow smoke. Gormy picked up the folded piece of paper. "Wait! That's secret! Get your paws off it!" protested Ruggle, but it was too late – Gormy unfolded it.

How to Stop Gormy Ruckles from Winning the Monster Boy Contest

(by Ruggle Ump)

Round 1 - Roaring

Just before Gormy is about to roar offer him a 'Boom Sweet' He'll think it's helping his roar, when it's a roar robbing Squeak sweet!

— SQUEAK!

Round 2 - Stomping

Fill Gormy's stomp sock with burning blister berries when he's not looking - his foot will be so HOT he'll never manage a proper stomp!

— AAGH!

FIRE

Round 3 - Throwing

Secretly paint a sleeping Goblouse rock-coloured, put Gormy's name on it and then carefully switch it for Gormy's Rock! Gormy will throw the Goblouse and the Goblouse won't like it one bit!

← Me

"What's going on, son? Did you do all those things?" asked a bewildered Brog Ump.

"Oh, fine, I admit it! I did it all! The squeak-sweet, the burning blister berries, even the goblouse!" cried Ruggle.

"But why? I thought we were friends," said Gormy.

"Friends? Hah! I was only *pretending* to be your friend so I could get close enough to mess things up for you!" yelled Ruggle, madly. "You see, I knew that you were the one monster boy monstrous enough to beat me. . ."

"But how? I've never even met you!" asked Gormy.

"Oh, but I knew all about you!" cried Ruggle. "When I won the *last* junior monster contest, I thought I was the most monstrous monster boy ever, but Poggy Boggles told me he knew someone even more monstrous – the most monstrous monster boy he'd ever met – *you*, Gormy Ruckles! Ever since then, I've been thinking up ways to mess up the contest for you!"

"Ruggle Thasslewinksytweed Ump, you cheated! You can't win by cheating!" cried Brog Ump. "Cheating isn't monstrous, it's . . . it's hoomum!"

"Don't worry, Brog, I'm sure Gormy could give Ruggle a monstering lesson or two," chuckled Grumbor.

Ruggle's father huffed and puffed with embarrassment. He sat Ruggle on a rock, and then made sure all the other monsters could hear him as he explained Ruggle's punishments for cheating. They included:

- **NO LEAVING HIS HOUSE ON BUTTERNUT HILL UNTIL HE WAS AT LEAST ONE TENTH-AND-A-SEVENTH**
- **NO GOATSHAKE, SHEEPSHAKE OR SLUGSHAKE EVER AGAIN**
- **FIFTY-FOUR LESSONS IN HOW TO BE LESS HOOMUM**
- **CLEANING THE DIRT AND GRUBS FROM BETWEEN GREAT GRANNY UMP'S TOECLAWS WITH HIS TEETH!**

. . .and thirty-two more. He was nearly at the

end when Ruggle shouted, "You can't make me!" and started scampering across the clearing at top speed.

"Gormy! Ruggle's getting away!" shouted Mike. Gormy didn't waste a second. He grabbed the curled-up goblouse and lifted it over his head.

"Hey Ruggle, catch!" he yelled, and threw the goblouse!

DWONK!

And the Winner is. . .

The goblouse soared through the air, curving in a perfect arc and landing right on top of the Ruggle's head. Ruggle fell flat on his face, dazed and defeated. Suddenly the Outspoken Oob appeared through the sea of monstrous legs and strode towards Gormy.

Gormy wondered if he was going to be in more trouble, but as he'd already been disqualified from the whole contest he wasn't too worried.

"GORMY RUCKLES, I SAW WHAT YOU JUST DID!" yelled the Outspoken Oob. "AND I MUST SAY, I HAVE NEVER SEEN SUCH MONSTROUS ROARING, STOMPING AND THROWING IN ALL MY DAYS! I HEREBY DECLARE YOU THE WINNER OF THE JUNIOR MONSTER CONTEST!"

"I . . . what? I won?" squealed Gormy.

"You won! Well done, my boy," said Grumbor.

Gormy had never won anything before! (Except that time that Mike bet him he couldn't eat a whole badger in one sitting.) As he swelled with monstrous pride, the Outspoken Oob retrieved the medals from a sore-headed Ruggle. He added the **Most Monstrous Throw** medal, and then hung all three around Gormy's neck.

"You did it, Gormy – you're the most monstrous monster boy in the land!" said Mike, proudly. As the other monster boys congratulated him, Gormy grinned so hard that his face started to hurt.

A moment later, he felt a snot-covered finger tap him on the shoulder.

"I *suppose* congratulations are in order," said a reluctant Poggy Boggles, as he wiped snot-gobs off his face.

"Thanks Poggy . . . and thanks for saving me from the goblouse," said Gormy.

"Well, I owed you that much. If I hadn't told Ruggle how monstrous you were, he would never have tried to mess up the contest for you," said Poggy.

"But why *did* you tell him I was monstrous? I thought you didn't like me," said Gormy.

"Hah! Just because I think you're monstrous, doesn't mean I *like* you," said Poggy, "and don't think just because I saved you that we're going to be friends either. Next time we see each other, it's business as usual."

"I wouldn't have it any other way," grinned Gormy.

Lesson six hundred and eleventy-twelve: A Little Monstrous Competition

As the sun began to set, Gormy, Mike and Grumbor set off for home. They made it back to Peatree Hill by morning, and Gormy wasted no time telling his mother all about his victory. She rewarded him with a mud-covered cow bar and two glasses of slugshake. Gormy was halfway through the second glass, when he realized how tired he was.

"Monstering can be a tiring business," said Grumbor, as Gormy yawned an exceptionally monstrous yawn. "You've earned a good night's sleep, just like you earned those medals. You're the only monster boy I know who could get disqualified and win a contest in the same day! I was very proud of you today. Now run along, tomorrow is another day for monstering."

With a broad grin, Gormy made his way upstairs and climbed into bed. He was still staring at his medals when Mike scuttied in through the window.

"I've never seen so many medals on one monster," he chirped.

"Glad to see you're feeling better – you look a lot less squashed than before," said Gormy.

He thought for a moment and added, "I'm sorry I didn't listen to you about Ruggle. I was so excited about being friends with a monster, I forgot that I've got the only friend I need."

"What? Who? You don't mean *Poggy Boggles*, surely! He's a. . . oh, wait! You mean *me*!" said Mike, blushing a deeper shade of slime-green. "Yeah, we do make a pretty good team don't we? I reckon every monster could use a scuttybug, especially when it comes to keeping an eye on the competition."

"Yeah, and we're going to do even better in the next contest," said Gormy. "I've learned my lessons – remember who your friends are . . . and try not to get eaten by a goblouse!"

MONSTER HERO

The Big Rain

It was a bright, cloudless afternoon in late Maytober, and Gormy Ruckles was busy thinking about tomorrow's monstering lesson. His father, Grumbor, had decided to test his knowledge of every one of his **How to be a Better Monster** lessons so far, from Lesson one-and-a-bit – Remember You're a Monster – to Lesson six hundred and ninety-nineteen – Never Forget You're a Monster.

Gormy wondered how he could possibly
remember everything he needed for the test. He
stared nervously out of the window, and spotted
his father standing on the front lawn. Grumbor
was one of the most monstrous-looking
monsters ever. He was bigger than ten cows tied
together and covered in thick, blue fur. As Gormy
wandered outside to join him, he noticed that

Grumbor was staring into the
sky and shaking his head.

"What are you looking
at?" asked Gormy.

"I felt a twinge in my
toeclaws," said
Grumbor. "*The Big
Rain* is coming."

"The Big Rain?

Really?" squealed Gormy, looking up. He couldn't see anything but clear, blue sky.

"My toeclaws are never wrong. Look there," said Grumbor, pointing to a single, grey cloud, growing larger and darker by the second. It swirled and churned as if it was alive. "And we all know what that means. . ." he added, grumpily.

"Uncle Kruckles is coming to stay!" Gormy shouted with glee, and ran back into the house. It was the most excited he'd been since he'd thrown his first rock! The Big Rain came at about the same time every year. More rain fell in one night than in all of the other nights put together. But it wasn't the rain that Gormy was excited about. It was the fact that every time the Big Rain came to the valley, so did his Uncle Kruckles!

"Mum, Uncle Kruckles is coming!" exclaimed Gormy again, as he dashed into the kitchen. His mother, Mogra, was busy preparing lunch. Mogra was almost as big as Gormy's father, but much more pink and a good deal jollier.

"I know, your father's been twiddling his toeclaws all day! Why do you think I'm cooking all this extra food?" she said, popping four just-

stomped goats into the oven. "You know how much Kruckles likes his goats."

Gormy felt like he was going to explode with excitement (which was rare but not unheard of amongst monsters).

As far as he was concerned, Kruckles Ruckles was the best uncle (and the best monster!) in the world. He was even more monstrous than Grumbor, with two ridiculously impressive horns and so much bright red fur that he could have donated half of it to the Society for the Bewigging of Balding Beasts and still been the hairiest monster ever.

What's more, Uncle Kruckles monstered wherever he wanted, whenever he wanted, and didn't let anyone tell him what to do. He didn't even have a house – he just slept in caves or under the stars, so that he never missed a chance to monster. Except when the Big Rain came – it was the one time of year Kruckles would seek shelter on Peatree Hill.

"He should be here any time now – he usually arrives before the Big Rain starts—" began Gormy's mother, but she was interrupted by a loud thunderclap. A second later, the skies opened and the rain began to fall.

"It's started! But . . . but he's not here! What if he's not coming?" cried Gormy, suddenly panicking.

"I'm sure he'll be here soon," said Mogra. "Now, why don't you go upstairs and check all the windows are shut, while we wait?"

Gormy raced upstairs, by now terribly concerned that Kruckles wasn't going to show up. Had he found somewhere better to stay? The thought was too horrible to contemplate. Gormy set about closing the windows, each time looking out to see if he could see Kruckles coming. He had just reached his bedroom window when he heard a small, gruff voice.

"Room for a small one? I'm close to drowning out here!"

"Mike!" said Gormy, as his best friend crawled in through the window. Mike was a scuttybug, and like all scuttybugs, he hated the rain, mainly because it tended to wash away any traces of his favourite food, poo.

"Is your uncle Kruckles here yet?" Mike asked as he scuttied on to Gormy's nose.

"No, and he always comes before the Big Rain! What if he's off on some amazingly monstrous adventure and he's forgotten all about us?" Gormy replied.

"Don't worry, Gormy – you know how Kruckles likes to make an entrance. He'll probably be here any second now," chirped Mike.

And a second later,

BOOOM!!!

Kruckles Ruckles

Something crashed through the ceiling! A massive shape fell to the floor next to Gormy, bringing most of the roof down with it!

"**Aaaah!**" screamed Gormy, leaping out of the way of the tumbling rubble. He scampered to the far corner of his room and crawled under a chest of drawers.

"What in the name of the Great Dung Heap was *that*?" squeaked Mike. "Is the sky falling in?"

"I don't know," whispered Gormy nervously, as the Big Rain poured in. In the centre of the room, he could see a huge, imposing shape. Gormy held his breath as it began to move.

"By the talking trees of Willow Wood, what a landing! I hope I didn't squash anyone important. . . " said a voice that sounded like hot lava flowing down a mountain. It was unmistakeable.

"Uncle Kruckles!" shouted Gormy.

"Gormy? That can't be you, can it?" said Kruckles as he got to his feet and dusted the debris out of his fur. "Look how much you've grown since I last saw you! Why, we're almost the same size!"

Gormy puffed up with pride at the thought

of having grown at all, but in fact, he was still no bigger than Kruckles' little fingerclaw. His uncle was even bigger than Gormy remembered – much taller than his father and at least twice as fat!

"What did you . . . how did you. . ." gasped Gormy, staring up at the enormous hole in the ceiling.

"What? Oh, yes, sorry I'm late. I was battling a family of dragons on Goggan Moor. Once we'd settled our differences I convinced one of them to give me a lift, so **WHOOSH!** off I went through the air! As soon as I spotted Peatree Hill below me, I hopped off and here I am!"

"You rode on a *dragon*?" cried Gormy, staring through the hole in the ceiling to see a long, snake-like dragon soaring across the rain-filled sky.

"Of course – it's the only way to travel! That reminds me, did I ever tell you about the time I battled the Seven Serpents of Sorrow Marsh?" Uncle Kruckles began, as Gormy's mother and father crashed into his room.

"Gormy! Are you all right? What happened?" cried Grumbor.

"Grumbor, you old rock-lobber! How about a hug for your not-so-little brother?" bellowed Kruckles, grabbing Grumbor and squeezing him tightly.

"Kruckles . . . so you did make it, after all," grumbled Grumbor. "Still making a mess wherever you go, I see. . ."

"Mogra, my dear! How do you put up with this grump? If you ever get sick of his belly-aching, you just let me know!" said Kruckles, with a wide, five-fanged grin. "And can it be? You look even *more* hideous than when I last saw you!"

"Oh, Kruckles, you sweet-talker," giggled Mogra, blushing a deep pink.

"Uncle Kruckles, this is my best friend, Mike," said Gormy, holding Mike up as high as he could. Kruckles leaned forward and squinted his eyes.

"What am I looking at, exactly?" he asked.

"Hello there," said Mike.

"A scuttybug!" exclaimed Uncle Kruckles. "Well, I'll be a monster's uncle! I bet you taste awful."

"I do, sir, I really do," said Mike, rather proudly.

"Excuse me," interrupted Grumbor, his ears steaming with rage. "But am I the only monster whose noticed that you've *wrecked Gormy's room*? There's rubble and water everywhere!"

"Oh, don't get your tusks in a twist, Grumbor – wrecking things is what monsters do. You don't mind, do you Gormy?"

"Nope!" said Gormy, happily, as a huge piece of ceiling rubble floated by his feet. As long as Kruckles was here, he didn't mind if the sky really did fall in!

"Well, all this monstrousness has given me an appetite! I could eat a dozen goats and still have room for snake pie!" bellowed Kruckles, slinging his sack over his shoulder.

"It's funny you should say that. . ." said Mogra, winking at Gormy.

Monsters Don't Need Lessons

Twenty-two minutes later, Uncle Kruckles had devoured (often without chewing):

- THIRTEEN ROASTED GOATS
- ONE PEELED COW
- SEVEN OTTERS-ON-A-STICK
- TWO GALLONS OF STOAT SOUP

- **FOUR PLATEFULS OF TOAD-IN-THE-HOLE**
  (made with real toads)
- **EIGHT SLICES OF SNAKE PIE**
  (with lashings of newt sauce)
- **HALF A HALF-BAKED HOOMUM**

Gormy had never seen any monster eat so much! Finally, Kruckles sat back in his chair and let out the almightiest burp Gormy had ever heard,

BUUUURR RUURU UOARUUP!!

"By the Cliffs of Lunacy, that was the most monstrous meal I've had all year – and last week I ate through a mountain!" said Kruckles, patting his huge red belly.

"So, how long are you planning on staying *this* time?" asked a disgruntled Grumbor.

"Long enough to spend some quality time with my favourite nephew, of course!" said Kruckles. "So, Gormy, how about tomorrow I take you on a proper monstering adventure?"

"An adventure? In the land beyond the hill?" squealed Gormy, his ears whistling with excitement. "That would be *amazing*!"

"Oh no you don't, Gormy Ruckles. You have a test tomorrow," said Grumbor, sternly. "Lesson seven hundred – The True Test of Monstrousness."

"But. . ." began Gormy.

"Lessons? You're not still bothering with that nonsense, are you?" laughed Kruckles. "Monsters don't need lessons! We're monsters, monstering is what we do naturally!"

"It's not that simple—" began Grumbor, angrily, but Kruckles interrupted.

"You know, Gormy, when your father was a monster boy, he used to spend all day with his snout buried in his **How to be a Better Monster** book. But not me! I didn't waste a second learning how to be a monster – I just got out there and did it!

And I turned out pretty monstrous, wouldn't you say?" Then he let out the most almighty **ROOOAARG!**

"You didn't have any monstering lessons? But you're the most monstrous monster *ever*!" said Gormy, easily as impressed as he was deafened.

"Ha! You're just saying that because it's true! So how about it, Grumbor? Don't you think it's high time that Gormy got to see the *fun* side of monstering? No books, no lessons, just some old-fashioned scaring and smashing?"

"I said no," said Grumbor, getting up from the table with a teeth-rattling thump. "What if you ran into a situation you couldn't handle?"

"Impossible! I can handle anything, and so

can Gormy . . . which reminds me, I forgot to give you your present!" said Kruckles, reaching for the large sack by his side. Gormy's eyes bulged with excitement – Uncle Kruckles' presents were always astonishing, unpredictable things from some far corner of a distant land.

His favourite presents so far were:

- **A TWISTED TRICK-STICK FROM THE KING OF THE HOP-GOBBINS**
- **A LOCK OF HAIR FROM THE ONCE-WAS-WICKED WITCH OF WORMLING COVE**
- **A TOOTH FROM POGUM OGUM, THE LIVING SWAMP**

Kruckles reached into the sack and rummaged around. "Aha – got it! Now close your eyes and hold out your paws!"

Gormy closed his eyes tightly and held his paws out. After a second, Kruckles shouted, "Open!" Gormy opened his eyes . . . and was confronted by an enormous bear!

"**Aaah!**" he screamed, as Kruckles dropped the bear on top of him!

He'd never seen a real, live bear before, never mind been squashed by one! It was three times bigger than he was, and at least four and a half times as heavy!

"Isn't he adorable? I thought he'd make a nice pet!" said Kruckles, cheerfully. "He's been in that sack for ages, so he'll be angry *and* hungry – a perfectly monstrous combination!"

The bear scrambled to its feet and began running around the kitchen, barrelling into a chair and knocking it over! Gormy leaped out of the way as the chair crashed to the ground in front of him.

"Well, he's certainly lively," said Mike, scuttying on to Gormy's shoulder.

"What were you thinking? You can't give

Gormy a bear!" growled Grumbor as he tried to catch it.

"Why not? A bear is the *perfect* present for a really monstrous monster boy, right Gormy?"

"I . . . I . . . yeah!" said Gormy. He had to admit, it was by far the best present he'd ever been given, even if it wouldn't stop crashing around the room. He decided that the polite thing to do would be to introduce himself to the bear (and hopefully calm it down a bit) so he leaped in front of its path and said, "Hello, my name's Gormy Ruckles. . ."

Unfortunately, this simply drove the bear to attack. It chased a screaming Gormy around the kitchen and out into the hall.

"See? He wants to play 'chase'!" added Kruckles.

Pursued by a Bear

After exiting the kitchen pursued by a bear,
Gormy raced through the hall, into the sitting
room, back out of the sitting room, and into the
study. The bear ran angrily after him, grunting
and growling.

"He's gaining on us!" cried Mike from
Gormy's shoulder. It struck Gormy that,
despite all his lessons, he still seemed to spend

more time running away from things than running after them! Maybe his uncle was right about lessons, after all. . .

"Go away! I'm not allowed any pets! Especially ones that try to eat me!" yelled Gormy as he darted into the study and ran around the enormous desk. The bear wasn't listening. It charged towards Gormy at full speed.

"Eaten by a bear . . . I can honestly say this is not how I thought it would end," said Mike with

a shrug. Gormy looked up at the enormous
bookshelf next to him. It was his only chance –
he leaped on to it and started climbing up the
books! He clawed his way up an enormous copy
of *Monstrous New World* and on to the next
shelf. Then he climbed up *Pride and
Monstrousness, Monstering Heights* and *Harry
Monster and the Goblet of Goats*. He was
halfway up a copy of *Coping With
Unmonstrousness* when he looked back. The
bear had started to climb as well! It dragged itself
up the books by its claws, and was moving at an
incredible speed!

"He's right behind us!" cried Mike, now a little nervous. Sure enough, the bear was only one book away! Without thinking, Gormy pulled the nearest book off the shelf.

"Hey, bear! How about a little light reading?" shouted Gormy, and threw the book!

KLOMP!

It landed on the bear's nose! The bear lost its balance and fell to the floor with a **THUMPH!**

A second later, Grumbor and Mogra burst into the room, closely followed by a chuckling Uncle Kruckles.

"There you are! Are you all right?" said Grumbor, grabbing the dazed bear in his massive claws.

"I'm . . . I'm great!" cried Gormy,

beaming from pointy
ear to ear. He'd never had
such a monstrous present in his entire life. It was
better than a million of Pogum Ogum's teeth
(which was nearly a whole mouthful). In fact, it
was probably the best present ever! "Can I keep
it? Can I?" he pleaded.

"What? No, of course not! You're not ready
for . . . for bears!" growled Grumbor.

"Of course he is! Gormy can handle
anything," said Uncle Kruckles, picking up the

book that Gormy had thrown at the bear. He chuckled and held it up. "And would you look at this! It looks like Gormy finally found a good use for monstering books!"

Gormy looked at the book. On the front it said: How to be a Better Monster by Grumbor Ruckles (aged one fifth and one sixth).

"And what's more," continued Kruckles, "I think he's proved that he's monstrous enough for a real adventure! What do you say?"

Gormy held his breath with anticipation, and crossed his claws.

"It couldn't hurt, you know," said Gormy's mother. "Gormy has been working very hard lately – he could probably afford to miss one lesson and have a little fun. . ."

"Please, Dad! I won't get into trouble, I promise!" begged Gormy. Grumbor sighed and rubbed his eyes.

"Fine," he said. "You can go with your uncle for one day and one night, and no more. After that it's straight back to the hill, and straight back to lessons."

"Thanks, Dad!" cried Gormy, beside himself

with excitement. "And can I keep my bear?"

"No! No bears! This is a house, not a zoo!" cried Grumbor. He looked around for somewhere to put the bear, but he couldn't see anywhere. He shrugged, popped it in his mouth and swallowed it whole.

The Adventure Begins

After a night full of monstrously adventurous
dreams, Gormy woke up feeling even more
excited than he did on Muffaluffmas Day (which
is like Christmas Day but all the presents are
alive). He hopped out of bed and jumped into
the pool of water that was once his room (his
father had patched the hole in his ceiling with
two trees from the garden, but it was still letting

in monster-sized drips) and packed his backpack for the adventure ahead. Then, after a breakfast of cow-tail crumpets, Gormy and his uncle, and of course Mike, set out on their adventure.

"Have a good time, my little furball," called his mother, as she and Grumbor waved them off. "And do *try* not to get into trouble."

"I won't!" said Gormy, rather hoping that he would.

"And if you run into problems, remember your lessons!" Grumbor shouted after them.

"Oh, stop fussing – Gormy's in safe claws with me! We'll be back by next sunrise!" boomed Kruckles.

As they set off down the hill, the ground was still wet from where the Big Rain had fallen. Gormy followed Uncle Kruckles through the ring of trees that surrounded Peatree Hill and emerged in the land beyond the hill. The valley had been turned into a river! Gormy could no longer see the bottom of the hill – in fact, he couldn't see the valley at all. It was completely submerged, with only the tops of the tallest trees poking out from beneath the water.

"How will we get off the hill?" said Gormy, suddenly worried that they would have to have their adventure in the garden!

"We're not going to let a little water stop us!" laughed Uncle Kruckles. He picked up Gormy and lifted him all the way up to the top of his head. "Hang on tight, we're going for a swim!"

Gormy barely had time to grab hold of Kruckle's head-fur before he began stampeding down the hill! Faster and faster he ran, until they were almost at the water's edge, and then he leaped into the air! Gormy held his breath and

SPOSHOOₒₒₒOOOₒₒOSH!!

They plunged into the water!

Gormy gripped Kruckles' fur for dear life as he was completely engulfed – he even saw a fish swim past his face! After what seemed like a fifth of forever (but was probably only a second or two), they bobbed back up to the surface. As Kruckles rolled on to his back, Gormy crawled down his face and on to his fat belly.

"Wha – what happened?" said Mike, crawling out of Gormy's backpack and spitting out a mouthful of water. "I thought I made it clear that scuttybugs and water don't mix!"

"That was great!" giggled Gormy, shaking the water off his fur like a wet dog. "Can we do it again?"

"All in good time, my boy. There's a whole world out there, and it's ours for the monstering!" said Kruckles, as they floated down the river of rain-water.

Gormy stared out at the flooded valley, then up at the faraway cliffs and mountains. The land

215

beyond the hill seemed bigger and more exciting than ever before.

"Where are we going, Uncle Kruckles?" he asked.

"To wherever the river takes us," laughed Kruckles. "To adventure!"

Cow-ball

Gormy, Mike and Uncle Kruckles had been floating down the river for most of the morning. They had travelled far further than Gormy had ever been. Gormy lay on Kruckles' belly, staring up at the clouds, as his uncle regaled him with tales of monstrous exploits. They always began the same way, but each one was more spectacularly monstrous than

the last. Gormy's favourites, in reverse order of monstrousness, were:

"That reminds me, did I ever tell you about the time I trampled ten towns in two days?"

"That reminds me, did I ever tell you about the time I out-yakked the Yakkum-to-Yak?"

"That reminds me, did I ever tell you about the time I accidentally ate the Ghost Dog of Grimsmoor?"

"That reminds me, did I ever tell you about the time I thumb-wrestled the fifty-fingered Frump?"

Kruckles was halfway through telling Gormy about the time he battled the Wiggly-Woo for a wasp sandwich when, **TRRRRrrrrrrURF!**

Kruckles had run aground! The river of rain had finally started to dry up, and Kruckles had come to a halt at the bottom of a small hill. Ahead of them the land was lush and green, and above them loomed a huge mountain.

"Well, well! It appears we have arrived!" boomed Kruckles.

"Arrived where?" asked Gormy, hopping off his uncle's belly as Kruckles stood up and stretched to his full height.

"Ha! As long as there's monstering to be had, who cares where we are?"

"But what about Lesson three hundred and threety-four – Care About Your Whereabouts?

219

Dad says a monster should always know where he. . ." began Gormy, but Kruckles wasn't listening – he'd seen something over the horizon.

"By the Crooked Claws of Krung! I spy some cows!" cried Kruckles, bounding towards a herd of brown-and-white cows, who had gathered under a large tree. "Time for a little cow-ball!"

"What's cow-ball?" asked Gormy, but Kruckles was already too far away to hear him.

"Whatever it is, I don't think it's going to be pretty," said Mike, scuttying out of Gormy's backpack and under a nearby leaf. "If you don't mind, I might sit this one out."

Gormy watched in amazement as Kruckles wrenched the large tree out of the ground. He spun it around his head and then, with an almighty swing, swatted a passing cow, launching it into the air!

"**MOOOOoooooooo!**" cried the cow as it went flying! Gormy almost fainted at the sheer monstrousness of it all!

"What are the rules?" he asked, as Kruckles chased after the terrified cows.

"Rules? There are no rules! We're monsters!" roared Kruckles. He grabbed a large bull by the horns and threw it at Gormy, crying, "Here, have a go!"

"Uh-oh. . ." squeaked Gormy as the bull flew towards him! He looked around for something to bat it with, but the only thing he could see was a tiny twig. He lifted it up in front of his face as he saw the bull's shadow fall over him. . . **BLOMF!**

"Gmmmf-mmf!" mumbled Gormy, squashed between the ground and the bull's enormous rump.

After a few moments, Kruckles lifted the dazed bull off Gormy and tossed it into a nearby field. He peeled Gormy out of the ground and cried, "Great catch! You're a natural at cow-ball!"

"Really?" asked Gormy, spitting out a mouthful of cow-hair. He looked back at the Gormy-shaped hole in the ground. "That was great! Can we do it again?"

Gormy and Kruckles played cow-ball until they were both exhausted. Gormy even tried his hand at batting (with a medium-sized branch) and after being kicked in the head three or four times, he got quite good at it. It was the most fun he'd had all year. There were no rules, no lessons, and nothing to learn. There was just adventure! He was finally starting to feel like a real monster.

Up Close and Hoomum

By mid-afternoon, all the cow-related monstrousness had given Kruckles an appetite, and he and Gormy settled down for a spot of lunch.

"Is this what you do every day?" said Gormy, as he watched Kruckles roast a cow's leg over an open fire.

"Of course," laughed Kruckles, taking a

massive bite. "I am a monster, after all."

"You make monstering look easy, that's for sure," said Mike, tucking into a cow pat dung-ball.

"It is easy, my foul-tasting little friend! When you're a monster, you just do whatever you like, whenever you like, and no one can do anything to stop you! Nothing's mightier than a monster – we're at the top of the food-chain!"

Gormy stared out over the land, and wondered why his father had never told him this. It turned out monstering was easy! He was just starting to question whether all his lessons had been a waste of time when he spotted something in the distance. Smoke, rising up from the ground at the base of the large mountain. He looked more closely, and realized that the smoke was coming from the chimney of a small house. In fact, there were *lots* of houses.

"Uncle Kruckles!" whispered Gormy with barely-controlled excitement. "Hoomums!"

"By the Bones of the Black Witch, I do believe you're right!" cried Kruckles. "What are we waiting for? Let's go and scare them witless."

"Really? N-now? In the daytime? But what

about Lesson two hundred and fivety-eight –
Be Frightful After Nightfall? Dad said I
shouldn't approach hoomums in the day
because—" began Gormy.

"Honestly, you'd think your dad didn't
want you to be a monster! I think it's high-
time the hoomums found out just how
monstrous Gormy Ruckles really is. . ."

Gormy followed his uncle as he strode
fearlessly towards the hoomum village. The
minute they saw Kruckles coming, the
hoomums started screaming and running around
in fear.

"Look at them go! Silly creatures. I never get
tired of watching hoomums panic!" cried
Kruckles, as he tramped into the village. Gormy
ran behind him as his uncle upturned horse-

227

carts, kicked down walls and tore the roofs off houses!

"It's a messy business, this monstering," commented Mike as they watched Kruckles leap into the air and belly-flop on to a hut.

"I know . . . isn't it *brilliant*?" squealed Gormy. *Uncle Kruckles must be the most monstrous monster ever!* he thought as Kruckles stomped off in pursuit of a terrified horse, leaving Gormy alone in the village.

"Uh, Gormy?" said Mike, tapping Gormy on the shoulder with a greasy leg. "You might want to have a look at this. . ."

Gormy turned around slowly. There, standing in front of him, were three hoomums. They didn't look like "silly creatures" at all, close-up. They were at least twice as tall as Gormy and very angry looking. They paced slowly towards him, talking to each other in hushed tones. Gormy couldn't tell what they were saying (hoomum talk is too ridiculous for monsters to understand) but they clearly meant to catch him.

"Um, isn't this usually the part where we run for our lives?" whispered Mike as the hoomums got closer, but Gormy kept his ground. He was tired of running away . . . from hoomums, from bears . . . and he wasn't going to run away any more! As the hoomums were about to pounce, he took a deep breath.

GRrRROOAAGgGGH!

It was the most monstrous roar he'd ever done! The hoomums ran away screaming and flapping their arms! Gormy could hardly believe it! He'd scared away not one but *three* hoomums, and he'd never even had a lesson in how to do it!

"How's it going, Gormy?" asked Kruckles, as he rambled back into the village, juggling a couple of horrified hoomums.

"That was great! Can we do it again?" said Gormy, proudly.

"That's the spirit! It's like I always say, when you're a monster, there's nothing you can't handle! But I think we've done about all the monstering we can do here. So, where do you want to go next?" said Kruckles.

Gormy stared up at the vast mountain and grinned. "To adventure!"

The cave of the Gloam

Gormy and Kruckles had been climbing up the mountain for almost an hour. By the time they reached the top (still laughing about how much they'd scared the hoomums), the sun had begun to set, bathing the whole land in a deep orange glow. They stared out across a vast mountain range, full of high, snow-capped peaks and dark, bottomless ravines.

"Uncle Kruckles, look!" shouted Gormy, as they made their way along the top of the mountain. There, staked into the ground, was a small sign which said,

"Who's the Gloam?" asked Gormy.

"Haven't a clue!" bellowed Kruckles. "But I don't see why we should beware him. I've never bewared anything!"

A few steps further on, they came across another slightly bigger sign.

"Sounds like a challenge to me!" laughed Kruckles.

Further on, they spied a third and fourth sign, and then more, and more, and *more*... and each one was more alarming than the last:

VENTURE NO FURTHER! THE GLOAM LIVES HERE!

WHAT ARE YOU, CRAZY? YOU'RE HEADING STRAIGHT FOR THE GLOAM!

CAN'T YOU READ? TURN BACK! YOU DON'T WANT TO MESS WITH THE GLOAM!

LOOK, YOU MIGHT BE A REALLY BIG MONSTER BUT YOU SHOULD STILL DEFINITELY NOT GO ANY FURTHER! I MEAN IT! THE GLOAM IS BAD NEWS!

In fact, by the time the sun had set, Gormy and Kruckles had counted *three hundred and nine* signs. They happily ignored them all and continued to the edge of a steep ravine, with a long drop into darkness. On the other side of the ravine was what looked like the entrance to a cave, and strung across the gap, was a thin, rickety-looking rope-bridge.

"What do you think?" said Kruckles as they stood at the edge of the rope-bridge.

"What have we got to be afraid of? We're monsters!" said Gormy boldly, and stepped on to the rickety bridge. **K-REEEAK!**

Gormy stopped in his tracks as the bridge creaked like an old door. He looked down between the flimsy wooden planks. The ravine was so deep that it didn't seem to have a bottom! He suddenly felt rather nervous, and gulped unmonstrously.

"It looks as sturdy as a rock! Let's go!" boomed Kruckles, and strode on to the bridge.

KREAK! KREAK! K-K- KRREEEAK!

Kruckles' massive weight shook the bridge as if it was in a tornado! Gormy held on to the bridge's ropes for dear life as it swayed and swung! Finally, Kruckles reached the other side, and the bridge began to settle. Gormy held his breath and scampered across to where Kruckles was waiting at the mouth of a huge, black cave.

"Right! Let's see what all the fuss is about, shall we?" asked Kruckles, and tramped fearlessly into the cave. Gormy was about to follow, but for some reason, he just stood outside, frozen to the spot. It was as if the world was standing still. Then suddenly, thick, black smoke began pouring out from within the cave!

"Well, that doesn't look too good," said Mike. Gormy tried to peer into the darkness, but it was darker than a storm cloud. Then came a deep rumbling, like a cross between growling and rolling thunder.

"That doesn't *sound* too good either," said Mike.

"Uncle . . . Uncle Kruckles? Are you there?" whispered Gormy, as the rumbling growl became louder and louder. Then, finally, he heard a voice from inside the cave. It was his uncle's.

"Gormy! RUN!"

The Gloam

Kruckles came running out of the cave, faster than Gormy had ever seen him move!

"Time to go!" shouted Kruckles. "I think that's enough adventure for one day!"

"What is it? What's wrong?" asked Gormy. A second later, he got his answer. From inside the cave, the Gloam appeared. It was the most monstrous thing Gormy had ever seen.

It was ten times larger than Kruckles, and had
more fangs than all of the monsters Gormy had
ever met put together. Its two huge, thick arms

looked like tree trunks, and its long, thick tail was covered in a hundred and fourteen spikes, each one bigger than Gormy.

If that wasn't monstrous enough, the Gloam was constantly surrounded by a cloud of darkness – with two white eyes which burned through the gloom.

"B-b-big . . . m-monster. . ." was all a terrified Gormy managed to whimper. Kruckles ran towards him, reaching out to pick him up, but the Gloam's massive claw swept down and knocked Kruckles to the ground! Kruckles bounced along the ground like a big hairy ball. He'd barely scrambled to his feet when the Gloam loomed over him.

"Uncle Kruckles!" cried Gormy.

"Run, Gormy!" he cried, as the Gloam glared

at him with its fireball eyes. In fact, the Gloam's stare was so monstrous that it made Kruckles' hair turn white! Then the beast opened its huge, shadowy jaws and,

GRAAAAAARH!

The Gloam's roar was deafening! It sounded like all the monsters of the world roaring at once as part of a sponsored roar, and it was easily the most monstrous thing Gormy had ever heard! In fact, it was *so* monstrous that it made Kruckles' hair fall out! He was completely bald!

"I have to do something!" cried Gormy as the Gloam

lifted its vast foot and held it above Kruckles'
head. It was going to squash him! Without
thinking, Gormy picked up a nearby rock and
threw it!

TONK!

It bounced off the Gloam's hide as if it was a
tiny pebble, but it was enough to get the beast's
attention. It fixed its burning glare on Gormy.

"I'll tell you what," said Mike, trying to stay
calm, "I reckon now would be a great time to do
that whole running away thing."

As the Gloam turned to face Gormy, it
swatted Kruckles into a nearby tree, and
Gormy's uncle fell limply to the ground. The
beast roared, spewing a cloud of inky darkness
into the air, and then charged towards Gormy!
Gormy turned and raced towards the bridge on

all fours. He could hear the Gloam's thunderous footsteps behind him, each one shaking the ground like an earthquake! Then, just as Gormy thought he might just make it to the bridge, the Gloam's massive foot crashed to the ground in front of him!

BOOOOM!

"**YAAH!**" screamed Gormy, darting to his left! The Gloam lifted his other foot and stomped again, and again and again

**– BOOM!
BOOM!
BOOM!**

– as Gormy weaved and dodged for his life! Gormy knew that

sooner or later one of the Gloam's stomps would squash him flat, if something worse didn't happen first! Then, as if on cue. . .

"Watch out for its tail!" cried Mike as the Gloam swung its massive, hundred-spiked tail along the ground! Gormy ducked as it whooshed over his head, but it was so enormous it created a gale, blowing Gormy up into the air!

"**YAAAH!**" he screamed again, flying through the air and landing in a nearby tree! He grabbed on to a branch and secretly hoped that the Gloam hadn't seen where he had landed.

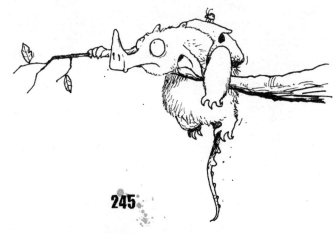

GRAAOOooOR!

roared the Gloam, making every leaf in the tree dry up and fall off. Gormy looked up to see the massive monster staring right at him.

"Uh-oh," he squeaked. The Gloam roared again and tore the tree out from its roots! It lifted the tree above its head and shook it until Gormy couldn't hold on any longer. . .

"**YAAAAAH!**" he screamed for the third time that day! He was flung out of the tree, through the air, and **KRUMP!** on to a rock! By now Gormy was dazed and aching, and would happily have lain there, rubbing his wounds, but the Gloam was already stomping towards him!

"Crushed by a giant monster . . . I think I'd

rather have been eaten by the bear," said Mike.

Gormy couldn't believe it – his first real monstering adventure and he was about to get eaten! It made him wish he'd stayed on Peatree Hill. He remembered sitting in the study with his **How to be a Better Monster** book, leafing through the pages and trying to remember every lesson . . . and then he realized that he did! Every single one, from one-and-a-bit to six hundred and ninety-nineteen – Gormy remembered them all! As the Gloam stomped towards him, an idea popped into his head.

"Lesson two hundred and two – Surprise Beats Size," he said to himself. He flexed his claws and gritted his teeth . . . and then did something very surprising.

He ran straight towards the Gloam!

10
Gormy Ruckles, Monster Hero

"Gormy! What are you *doing*?" screamed Mike, as Gormy ran towards the Gloam!

"I'll tell you later . . . if we make it out alive!" said Gormy. He took a deep breath into all four of his lungs and roared his most monstrous roar!

ROOAAAAAARGH!

The Gloam suddenly stopped in its tracks, and looked a bit confused! This was the first time anything had ever run *towards* it — usually everyone ran away — and this was certainly the first time anything had roared at it! The befuddled beast staggered back, not knowing what to think about this brave little monster. Perhaps it was so monstrous that it didn't *need* to be big! Gormy kept roaring and running towards the Gloam until it had staggered all the way back into its cave!

"I did not see that coming," said Mike with a surprised grin.

"He won't be gone for long – Lesson three hundred and seventy-eleven – Monsters are Never Gone for Long," said Gormy, skidding to a halt next to his uncle. "Uncle Kruckles, wake up! We have to go!" he shouted, prodding Kruckles with his paw.

"AAAAAH! BEWARE THE GLOAM!" screamed Kruckles, waking up. Then he looked down at his fat, bald belly and screamed again. "My fur! My precious fur! I'm naked!"

"We'll deal with that later!" said Gormy, helping Kruckles to his feet. They rushed to the rickety rope-bridge, and then made their way across **KREAK KREAK KREEAK!** as fast as they could. They were nearly halfway across when the sky darkened around them. . .

"He's back!" cried Mike. Gormy looked back to see the Gloam reappear from its cave and charge towards them! Gormy tried roaring again, but this time the Gloam kept coming. Within seconds it had reached the bridge!

KREAK KREEAKK KREEEAK! CRACK! KREEEEEAK! KRACK!

Gormy held on tightly as the bridge rocked and swayed with the Gloam's every clawstep! The fragile planks shattered beneath it, and one of the two ropes holding up the bridge snapped under the beast's weight!

"By the Bottomless Pit of Bottomless Bottoms!" yelled Kruckles as the bridge swayed from side to side. "There's only one rope left! If the Gloam breaks that, the bridge will split in two – we'll fall!"

"So, if the Gloam doesn't kill us, the fall will? Yikes!" gasped Mike. Gormy glanced at the last remaining rope, then at the Gloam, who was only seconds away.

"Lesson ninety-nine and a half – Never Fail to Use Your Tail!" he said, wrapping his tail tightly around the remaining rope. He nodded to Kruckles to do the same.

"By the Eighty Armpits of Ong!" cried Kruckles, realizing what he was planning. He wound his tail nervously around the rope and held his breath.

"Gormy, I hope you're not thinking what I think you're thinking!" said Mike.

"Hang on, Mike, we're going for a ride," he whispered, as the Gloam reached out a huge, black claw to grab them. Gormy stared straight into the beast's fiery eyes and clenched his little blue paws.

"Hey Gloam! Here's a lesson for you! Lesson five hundred and fivety-five – Expect the Unexpected!" he cried. Then he bared his one quite good fang, and bit through the rope!

"**YAAAAAHH!**" screamed Gormy. The bridge

split in two, sending Gormy and Kruckles crashing into the cliff-face with a **THRUMP!** The Gloam tried to leap for the side of the ravine, but it was too late – it fell, roaring an impossibly loud roar which faded into silence as it disappeared into the abyss.

Before long, Gormy and Kruckles had clambered up what remained of the broken rope-bridge, and out of the ravine.

"You did it!" squealed Mike, poking his head back out of Gormy's backpack.

"I *did* do it, didn't I?" said Gormy to himself, surprised at his own monstrousness.

"By the Hairy Eyes of Horg. . . I'm sorry I got us into such a mess, Gormy. I suppose there really *are* some things that are too monstrous for me to handle," said a regretful

Kruckles, but then he noticed that Gormy
had an enormous grin on
his face.

"That was great!" said
Gormy. "Can we do it again?"

11

Lesson Seven hundred:
The True Test of
Monstrousness

The trip back to Peatree Hill took the whole night and another whole day. By the time they got back, Gormy's mother and father were beside themselves with worry.

"Gormy, where have you been?" cried Mogra, squeezing him so tightly he thought he might pop.

"And why has your uncle Kruckles got no hair?" asked Grumbor.

Before long, all the important questions had been answered. After being given a thorough telling off for being so irresponsible, Kruckles settled down for a nap, carefully wrapped in a thick blanket to cover his hairless belly. Then, as Gormy's mother prepared hot goat juice for everyone, his father sat him down next to the fire.

"That was a very monstrous thing you did, saving your uncle from the Gloam," said Grumbor. "I always feared that one day Kruckles would get into a situation that he couldn't handle, but I didn't think it'd be *you* getting him out of it! Perhaps you are a little more monstrous than I give you credit for."

"I'm just glad I remembered all my monstering lessons when I met the Gloam," said Gormy.

"Glad to hear it. Then it sounds like you're

ready to take the True Test of Monstrousness!" said Gormy's father.

"The *test*? But – but I thought, I mean, after everything—" began Gormy, suddenly nervous.

"He's only joking – you don't need to take the test! You've more than proved how well you know your lessons," said his mother, handing him a cup of goat juice. "You've made us both very proud, Gormy."

"What's more, we think you've proved that you're ready for some *real* monstering," said his father, resting a large claw on Gormy's shoulder.

"Really? Out there, in the land beyond the hill?" Gormy asked, excitedly.

"Absolutely! I might come along too, though – just to make sure you don't get into *too* much trouble," chuckled his father. "So, where do you think you'd like to go first?"

Gormy took a sip of goat juice, and grinned an exceptionally monstrous grin. "To adventure!"

LOOK OUT FOR MORE FROM GUY BASS

MORE MONSTER MISHAPS STARRING GORMY RUCKLES

BLUE PETER
WINNING
AUTHOR
BOOK AWARD

BEWARE:
Contains scary monsters and slime!

MONSTER
MADNESS

GUY BASS

ALSO BY GUY BASS

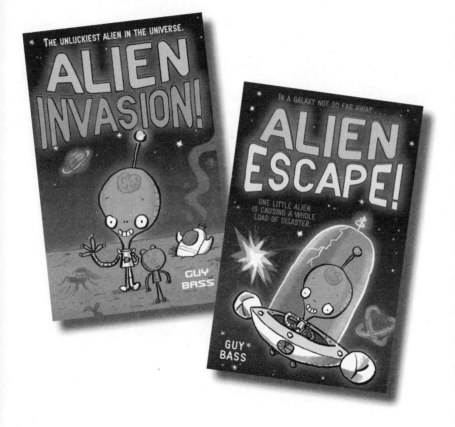

COMING SOON...